Elias

AMY AISLIN

ALSO BY
Amy Aislin

STICK SIDE SERIES
On the Ice
The Nature of the Game
Shots on Goal
Risking the Shot

WINDSOR, WYOMING SERIES
Home for a Cowboy

LIGHTHOUSE BAY SERIES
Christmas Lane
Gingerbread Mistletoe

LAKESHORE SERIES
The Heights

OTHER BOOKS
Ballerina Dad
The Play of His Life
As Big as the Sky

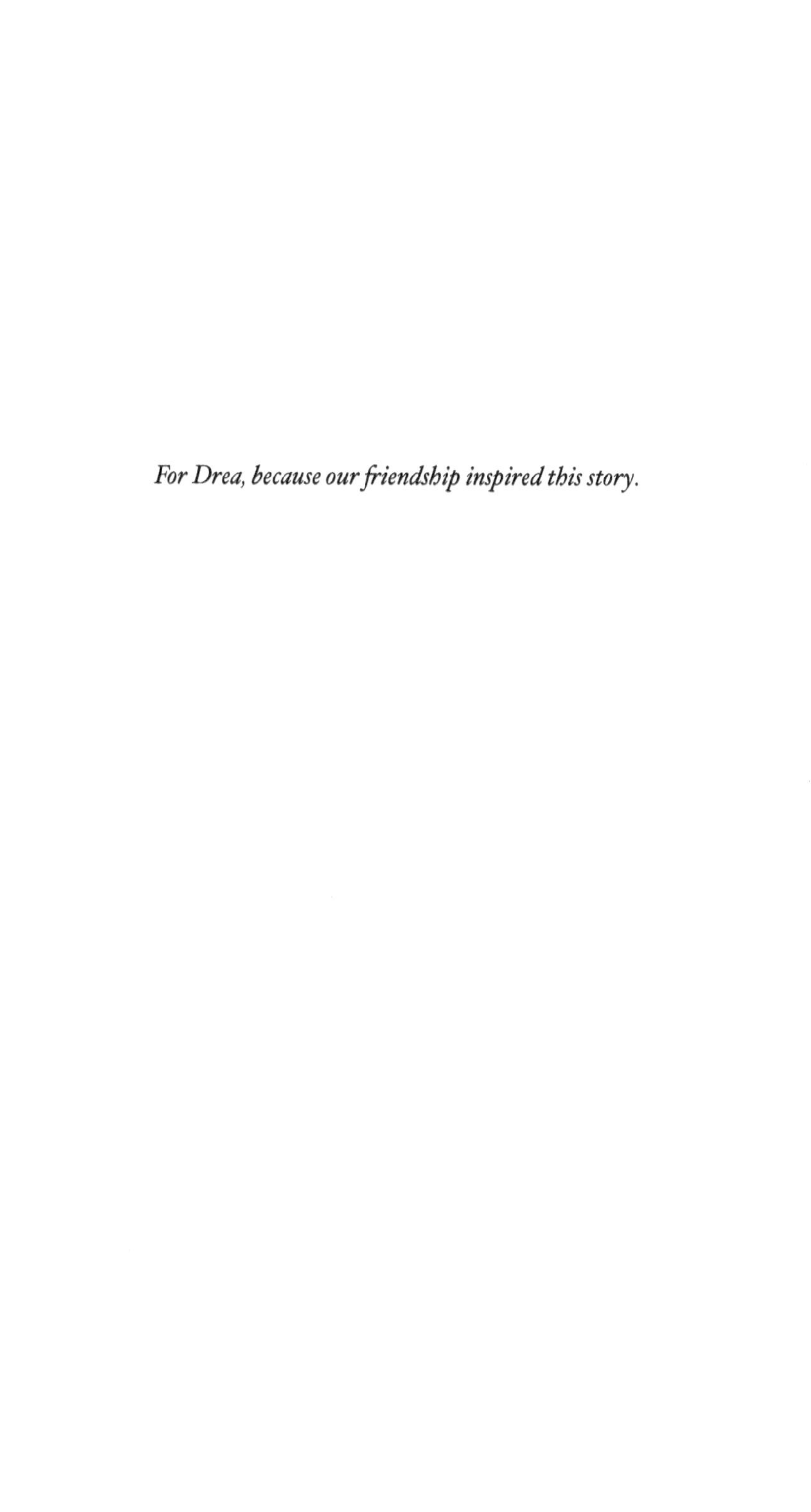

For Drea, because our friendship inspired this story.

Chapter One

Week two of the new year, and you're back in the groove after a stressful holiday season, Capricorn. Be nice to others this week. You never know where it could lead.

PFFT. *BE NICE TO OTHERS?* WHAT KIND OF HOROSCOPE WAS that? He could get a better reading from a fortune cookie.

Elias Hood tugged the scarf around his neck higher, covering his mouth and nose, and secured his toque more snuggly over his ears. Head down against the brutal blizzard, he trudged his way up Bay Street, boots marking a path behind him that was almost instantly swallowed up by the blowing snow.

Be nice to others. He was always nice to others. It wasn't his fault he had resting bitch face—or 'resting douchebag face' as Rachel called it. Even when he was in a shit mood, he was nice to others. All right, so that last part wasn't strictly true, but he avoided people when he was in a shit mood. That had to count for something, right?

He didn't bother looking up until he reached Wellington Street and only then to make sure the light was green. It wasn't. Elias waited with the other three pedestrians for the light to turn. Normally, at this time of the morning, the sidewalks were crawling with fancy-suited, briefcase-carrying commuters rushing to work. Today, people smarter than him were either working from home or calling in sick. He already had six emails from staff who weren't coming into the office. The streetcars weren't running. The subway was delayed. Commuter trains were cancelled. Streets hadn't been plowed.

The roads were icy. The kids had a snow day. Elias didn't have an excuse. He lived within walking distance to his office, but even had that not been the case, he would've come in anyway. Showing up on such on awful morning showed commitment and respect and trust.

It might just be enough to get him that promotion to VP.

But God, winter in Toronto sucked big, frozen, ice-cream balls. The snow wasn't the soft, Christmassy-looking type that fell gently and made everything look pretty. No, it was raining ice pellets, sideways no less. The wind was so strong that it dislodged fist-sized clumps of snow from rooftops and bus shelters and awnings, sneaking around buildings hard enough to throw what felt like enormous, ice-encased snow-balls into his face.

Stepping into the intersection, he crossed the street with his fellow dedicated commuters.

"Sorry," he muttered, when he accidentally bumped into someone going in the other direction. See? He could be nice.

Bunching up the morning newspaper with its useless advice column masquerading as a horoscope, he tossed it into the next trash can he passed.

"Hey!"

It was less windy on this side of the street, the tall down-town buildings a buffer against the wind. He jammed his gloved hands into his jacket pockets and—

"Hey!"

Elias turned. A guy dressed in a huge, puffy, white jacket with an orange-and-yellow city-worker vest over top scowled at him from next to a series of trash cans. Like Elias he had his scarf up over his mouth and nose, toque over his ears. His ice-blue eyes were so frosty they would've frozen Elias's balls had the blizzard not already done that for him.

"Paper goes in this one." The city worker pointed at one of the cans. He was about Elias's height, roughly five feet ten.

Other than that Elias couldn't tell much about him in his snowman outfit. He could've been a skinny beanpole or a gym rat, twenty years old or fifty.

"Huh?"

The guy lowered his scarf, uncovering his nose and mouth. "Newspapers," he said slowly like he was talking to an idiot. "They go in *this* can."

Elias looked at the can in question. *Recycle*, it said with a picture of a newspaper, a ticket stub, and one of those triangular pieces of cardboard every pizza place ever served their pizza slices on. The next can also said *Recycle*, but had a picture of pop cans, water bottles, and milk cartons. The third trash can said *Litter*, which probably meant everything else was supposed to go in there.

Wait. Was he being schooled on how to sort his garbage properly?

"What does it matter?" Elias asked. "Doesn't it all go to the same place?"

The guy huffed, the breath he expelled clouding around him.

"No. Paper, plastic, metal, and glass all get separated and recycled for different purposes."

City Worker kept talking, but Elias stopped listening. He didn't care what happened to his garbage, as long as it got picked up once a week.

"You know what?" Elias interrupted the guy's monologue on glass plants and plastic plants and what-the-fuck-ever plants and made a show of peering at his watch. "I'm late. I gotta..." He turned and left.

Because seriously? He didn't need this on a Monday morning. He was twenty minutes late already, most of his staff weren't coming into the office, his toes were freezing, and he couldn't feel his nose.

By the time he got to his office building at Bay and King a

few minutes later, the bottom of his pants were soaked, his face was stinging, his nose was running, his fingers were stiff, and he had two more emails from staff who were working from home.

Which, everyone knew, was a euphemism for napping and binge-watching Netflix.

A new email came in as he was booting up his computer in his office. Fingers still achy, he fished his phone out of his pocket.

Dear Mr. Hood,

Thank you for your submissions to CanadaTravels *magazine. Your Algonquin Fall Colours photo will be used on the cover of our September issue; the six others you submitted will be used in a four-page feature story about fall camping in Algonquin Park. Please find contract details enclosed and....*

Ha! That made four editions of *CanadaTravels* magazine that would feature his photos this year. He tapped the pdf icon on his phone to open the contract, but Rachel appeared in his doorway—like she did every morning between eight and nine—before he had a chance to skim it.

"I didn't expect you today," he said.

"I live down the street." Rachel deposited herself in one of his visitor's chairs. "It'd be pretty sad if I couldn't make it in." She quirked an eyebrow. "So?"

"So?" he evaded. Rachel was his best work friend. They didn't interact outside of the office, but here they got along like a couple of teenage best friends.

Rachel rolled her eyes heavenward. "What did it say today?"

"Nothing useful." Elias set his phone aside and logged into the internal system on his computer. "Told me to be nice to people."

"Hmm." Rachel tapped her lips with a pink fingernail. "And have you been?"

"I'm always nice."

Rachel cracked up.

Confused—and maybe a little bit hurt—he looked at her around his computer screen. "Why is that funny?"

"Oh my God. Oh my God, you actually believe that." She looked like she was about to fall on the floor she was laughing so hard.

"I *am* nice," Elias defended himself. He realized he hadn't exactly been nice to the city worker giving him shit this morning, but that was just a one-off.

"I don't know if 'nice' is what I would call you," Rachel said, laughter still in blue eyes almost the exact same shade as the city worker's. And why was he even thinking about that? "'Tenacious' and 'determined' are what I would call you." Elias didn't think it was a compliment. "'Responsible. Practical. Organized.'"

"You're describing a robot."

He'd clearly startled her. "No, no, I don't mean it in a bad way," Rachel said, serious for once. "They're all good things."

Sure didn't sound like it.

"Anyway, I'd listen to your daily horoscope."

"Why?" Elias asked. "It's all a bunch of hocus pocus bull-shit anyway."

Rachel's jaw tightened at his usual response. "Anyway, the reason I came in here. My cousin is visiting this weekend. He's twenty-nine and single and gay and..." She paused for dramatic effect. "He's a Taurus," she sing-songed.

"Why does that last part matter?"

"Oh my God." Rachel flopped back in her chair, flinging her arms wide. "Have I taught you nothing? Taurus is one of Capricorn's most compatible signs."

"Why?" Not that he cared. He was just curious.

"You're both pragmatic and rational, both have the same seriousness, treat life the same way."

There she went with the robot description again.

"Capricorn and Taurus are basically the same, then?"

Rachel literally face-palmed. Her hand smacked her forehead, and she wilted in her chair. "Why do I bother? I'm done. You're hopeless." She took her pant-suited self toward the door. "Don't fire too many people today," she called over her shoulder before disappearing. She poked her head back in. "Let me know by the end of the week if you want to meet Steve."

"I can tell you right now," he called even though he couldn't see her anymore. "The answer's no!"

Him on a blind date? There was almost nothing he wanted to do less.

The weather's looking up, Capricorn, and so are you. Don't forget to treat people the way you like to be treated. Karma always notices a good deed.

"HERE YOU GO."

City Worker blinked at the coffee cup Elias held out, eyeing it with suspicion. Dressed once again in a huge, white, puffy jacket, maroon scarf, and orange-and-yellow vest, he'd foregone the toque today. After a full week of the temperature hovering somewhere in the negative twenties, today was only minus five, which felt downright warm by comparison. Elias had left his own toque at home.

"What is it?" City Worker asked, making no move to reach for the proffered cup.

"It's coffee," Elias said. "With a touch of milk, since I don't know how you take it."

This was the lamest I'm-sorry gesture ever. He didn't believe in horoscopes and zodiac signs and whatever, but if the universe wanted him to be nice, he'd be nice. Plus, he normally didn't treat people the way he'd treated this guy yesterday, and he did feel bad about it. It'd just been windy and nut-freezingly cold and snowing ice pellets of doom. Combined with most of his staff taking the day off due to the blizzard, he'd perhaps been a touch cranky.

City Worker's face folded in confusion. Still he didn't take the cup. His hair was blond, both on his head and on his unshaven jaw, and he had dark roots and dark eyebrows. The hair didn't appear dyed though; it was more like his genes couldn't decide if he should be blond or brunette and he'd gotten a bit of both. Probably somewhere in his mid-twenties, his soft face made him look eighteen, yet the full lips and frosty eyes gave him a certain maturity.

"Why?" City Worker asked.

"It's an apology," Elias explained, promptly realizing he hadn't yet apologized. "I'm sorry about yesterday. I was a dick, walking away like that. And here." He took the rolled-up newspaper from the back pocket of his leather messenger bag and delivered it into the correct *Recycle* trash can. "See?" He could be cooperative.

City Worker wasn't impressed.

Fed up, Elias thrust the cup at the unappreciative guy, who had to take it in a gloved hand otherwise it would've spilled all over his pristine white coat. Out of his own coat pocket, Elias extracted a few mini creamers and milks and several sugar packets—raw, brown, and white. He was considerate that way.

"In case you need extra," he said and thrust them into City Worker's other hand. Nodding in satisfaction, Elias continued his walk to his office, feeling quite proud of himself.

It's another cold one today, Capricorn! But it'll be sunny at least, so don't forget your sunglasses. Speaking of sun...why not try and brighten someone's day?

"Is hot chocolate more your thing?"

City Worker finished replacing the garbage bag in one of the trash cans before turning to Elias. Elias had to squint—he *had* forgotten his sunglasses, damn it. City Worker didn't have the same problem, his eyes hidden behind a pair of functional sports sunglasses. Which was really too bad—not only were his eyes a really impressive light blue, but the sunglasses meant Elias couldn't see where he was looking or what expression his gaze might hold. Although the wrinkled brow and the mouth set in a tight line gave him a good guess.

"You didn't seem too impressed by yesterday's coffee."

Not that he seemed all that impressed by today's hot chocolate either. Why was Elias still trying? He'd apologized already. And he didn't need to take the extra twenty minutes to stop at a café on the way to work to get something for City Worker. But it made him feel good to be doing something for someone else. Not to mention it must suck like the ass-crack of dawn to work outside all day in this the cold weather. A warm drink could only make the whole prospect a little bit bearable.

And yeah, he was kidding himself. City Worker was a young, tall, smoking-hot blond who was completely Elias's type except for the no-talking thing. Elias usually went for guys who spoke back to him, but it was fine. He could hold the conversation for both of them. Maybe. For about twenty seconds.

"Here." Elias took a step forward, getting out of the way of the massive throng of morning commuters, and held out the cup in his hands. To his surprise, City Worker actually took it today.

He was still scowling when Elias walked away, but when Elias turned back before he entered his office building, it was to see the city worker taking a large gulp of his drink.

Get out of your comfort zone, Capricorn, and do something new today.

"Do you like apple turnovers?"

Another fucking cold day, another out-of-the-way stop at the café. Elias held the paper bag out to City Worker. Everybody liked apple turnovers. Maybe this time his offering would actually get City Worker to talk to him.

Elias felt monumentally stupid and more and more like he should just give up. So this guy was his type, so what? There were plenty of other tall, blond guys in a city of two-point-six million. He just had to walk on over to The Village—Toronto's predominantly gay neighbourhood at the intersection of Church and Wellesley—to find one. And he'd done that on occasion, but it had only resulted in him feeling unsatisfied and lonely and used up. One-night stands just weren't his thing.

Plus City Worker actually gave him butterflies, which hadn't happened since his stupid one-sided crush on Ben Croll in ninth grade.

City Worker had abandoned the sunglasses today—it was overcast and threatening snow again—so Elias registered the brief flare of amusement that warmed those blue eyes from icy winter to hot summer sky before City Worker carefully schooled his features.

"You've been playing me!" Elias exclaimed.

His words had City Worker throwing his head back in a laugh. His smile was wide and white, eyes crinkling at the corners. Damn if Elias's butterflies didn't flutter in simpering puppy love.

"I'm sorry," City Worker said, grin belying his words. "But you come over here all serious even as you hand me an apple turnover? You look like the world is ending."

That was Elias's resting douchebag face at work. He was probably wearing it even now.

"I'm Ty," City Worker said, thrusting out a hand. His voice was pleasantly modulated and smooth, but it sounded young. Elias reassessed his mid-twenties estimate. Maybe this guy really was eighteen.

That would be unfortunate. Elias was a long way past his teenage years.

Nevertheless, after introducing himself and shaking Ty's hand, he took his horoscope's advice and did something new.

"Do you want to grab a coffee?"

Chapter Two

Sitting across from Elias at a small table at the back of a local coffee shop, Ty chuckled to himself. This was the funnest week he'd had in a long time. The thought made him realize how pathetic he was, that taking the piss out of a stranger for a few days was the highlight of his uneventful life.

Elias had delivered his apple turnover and his hot chocolate and his coffee with such a dour expression on his face the past three days that Ty hadn't been able to resist toying with him. And admittedly the warm drinks had been a plus.

Although this invitation for coffee had come as a surprise. Hopefully it would help Elias get that uncomfortable-looking stick out of his ass.

"You didn't have to buy me coffee," Elias said now. "I invited you. I should be paying."

"It was the least I could do after the past few days," Ty said, sipping his hot chocolate. Elias had gotten that one right. Ty hated coffee. He'd only had a few sips of the one Elias had brought him.

As Ty swallowed another sip, Elias gave him a blatantly obvious once-over that was, sadly, more curious than sensual.

"How old are you?" Elias asked.

Ty's eyebrows went up at the question. "Twenty-six."

Now it was Elias's eyebrows that went up. "Are you sure?"

"Do you want to see my driver's license?" Ty asked, chuckling.

"It might be a fake," Elias said with a slight smirk.

"I haven't had a fake since high school," Ty said. He split

the apple turnover in two and handed one half to Elias. "It was my older brother's. I only used it twice, though. I've never been a big drinker, and clubbing was never my thing."

"I never had one," Elias admitted. "Too afraid to get caught."

Elias looked his age, ruggedly handsome in a lawyer-type way. He was clearly a businessman—his dark blue suit was tailor-made, and his brown leather messenger bag was buttery soft. He had warm, café-au-lait skin, dark brown eyes, and black hair gelled into a short faux-hawk. His face was long and patrician, but the short, neat beard kept him from looking too much like a lawyer. In fact, he looked like an outdoor enthusiast-cum-lawyer.

He was beautiful in an imposingly masculine way. Ty wouldn't want to meet him in a court room.

Elias's phone sat on the table next to his coffee cup. God, Ty hated when people did that. Like, *Hello! I'm sitting right here!* Even as he had the thought, Elias's phone lit up, and he glanced at it.

"So tell me," Ty said, before Elias could check his new message. "What kind of lawyer are you?"

Elias blinked at him. "I'm not a lawyer."

"Are you sure?" Ty teased, mimicking Elias's earlier question.

It made Elias laugh, and eeeeee gods! Damn, but no one should have a smile that killer. He probably had pretty boys falling at his feet. Ty had been called a pretty boy once or twice or a dozen times. It made him want to hit someone every time.

"I'm sure," Elias said. "I work for Top Line, Ltd. Basically we get called in to assess things when a company goes through a reorganization."

The smile slipped off Ty's face. Yeah, he knew all about reorganizations. His dad had felt the effects of a reorganization when Ty was a kid. "Reorganization" was a fancy word for "layoffs."

"Hi there!" A barista stopped next to their table, holding a tray of mini plastic cups filled with dark liquid. "We're sampling our new dark-chocolate espresso flavour today. Would you like one?"

Ty declined; Elias took one. The blissed out look on his face once he swallowed? Mouth slack, eyes wide and pleased? Ty tried not to imagine Elias wearing that expression during an orgasm and failed epically.

"What do you do?" Elias asked.

Redirecting his attention off Elias's mouth, Ty took a sip of hot chocolate to wet his dry throat. Elias was much too hot, much too put together, much too confident. It made Ty feel like an inexperienced teen, especially dressed as he was in baggy jeans, a white thermal top, and an open flannel shirt. "I work for the city. I cover about a four-block radius, removing trash and replacing garbage bags in public garbage cans as well as in some commercial buildings."

Elias was nodding. "Cool," he said. It was a pretty typical response to Ty's job. Nobody ever seemed to know what to say when Ty told them he was a garbage man. It wasn't a glamorous job, but somebody had to do it. And Ty liked it. He got to spend most of his day outside, he made good money, and he worked decent hours with a great crew.

Elias went silent again, so Ty went with one of his favourite getting-to-know-you questions.

"Do you have any pets?"

"No."

Huh. That question usually elicited a longer response.

"I had a hamster when I was a kid," Elias finally elaborated after taking a sip of his coffee. "Does that count?"

Ty couldn't stop his charmed smile. "Sure. What was his name?"

"Booger."

Ty snorted his drink. Fuck, it hurt! Holy mother, who knew getting hot chocolate up the nose would burn so badly? His eyes watered on top of everything, and it probably looked like he was either crying or laughing himself to death.

He needed to blow his nose, and the tiny one-ply café napkins would never do and—

"Here." Elias thrust a travel pack of tissues in his face. Oh, thank Christ. Ty had left his own travel pack in the console of his waste-removal truck—which was in the parking lot around the corner.

Once he'd blown his nose, he glanced at Elias—who looked like he was biting his cheek to hide his smile—crumpled up the tissue in his hand, and said, "Speaking of booger..."

Elias's laugh was soft, like he was having trouble believing the conservation was actually happening.

"Sorry," he said. "I didn't mean to make you..." He waved at Ty like, *choke on your drink and almost die*.

"No biggie," Ty said. "Not your fault. I just didn't expect...Booger. It's not what I would've pictured you naming your hamster."

"What name did you think I'd go for?"

Ty narrowed his eyes on him and made a show of pretending to think it through, stroking an imaginary beard. "Apple."

"That's..." Elias seemed to think about it. "That's a pretty good name for a hamster, actually."

"I'm awesome at naming pets," Ty admitted.

Elias grunted. "You should put that on your resume."

Ty laughed, his entire body warming under Elias's teasing. It was an unexpected yet thoroughly enjoyable change from his attitude pre-Booger. *This* Elias was smiling softly, bantering with him, ignoring his phone—which was blowing up on the table next to him. Ty should probably point it out —Elias might be needed somewhere urgently—but he was enjoying his company too much.

"Do you live in the city?" Elias asked.

"For now," Ty said. "I bought a house recently. Took possession last week, actually. I move on Saturday." He didn't mention that he was still living at home—because that was just sad—or that he couldn't wait to get away from his well-meaning yet large, loud, and nosy family.

"Congratulations!" Elias toasted him with his mug, a wide smile creasing his cheeks. "Do you need help moving? I'd be happy to help."

Ty sat back in his chair and chewed the last bite of his apple turnover. Elias was hot, no question. But ever since they'd sat down, he'd looked sometimes uncomfortable, sometimes at a loss for words. Did he regret asking Ty out for coffee? Maybe he was uncomfortable with people he didn't know?

Either way, his offer to help came as a surprise seeing as they barely knew each other. Ty almost told him he had enough people willing to lend him a hand on the weekend, but it'd be nice to get to know Elias, maybe go on a few dates, see where things led.

"Sure," he finally said. "I could always use an extra hand."

Chapter Three

As of 5:00 pm last Friday, Ty was the proud owner of a small, two-storey, three-bedroom home in Puslinch. Built in the mid-seventies, it was just over sixteen-hundred square feet on a third of an acre of land that looked like his own private park. His nearest neighbour owned a horse farm half a kilometre south. To the north, the street dead-ended at a regional conservation area.

There were streams and rivers nearby and plenty of hiking trails. It was quiet, and yet it was only a fifteen-minute drive to downtown Guelph.

It was perfect. It was all his. And best of all? It was over an hour's drive away from the rest of his family on a good day. On a bad day—which in the Greater Toronto Area's crazy-ass traffic was almost every day—it would take nothing short of a Mack truck running over their house to convince his parents, his brothers and sisters, his grandparents, his cousins, and his aunts and uncles to make the trip here for anything but a pre-planned family gathering. *And* he wouldn't be called up on a whim to babysit his nieces and nephews.

He loved his family, but God, did he ever need his space.

"Dude, where do you want this?"

His older brothers held his bedroom dresser between them.

"Upstairs," Ty instructed. "Bedroom on the left. It says so on the sticky note taped to the top." He followed behind the twins, watching them sweat their way up the stairs to the second floor, cussing the entire time.

It had taken Ty an embarrassingly long time to decide

which bedroom he wanted for himself. The master bedroom on the first floor had huge windows and a set of patio doors that led nowhere—the previous owners never got around to building a deck. The upstairs bedrooms were two feet smaller than the master, but the room on the left of the stairs had a window seat.

"Maybe I should've taken the master downstairs," he muttered. Right as his brothers set the dresser down in his room upstairs.

"Oh, fuck that," Matt said.

"Not this again." Jeremy rolled his eyes.

"We are *not* lugging this thing back downstairs."

"Notice he didn't even help us get it up here?" Jeremy said to Matt. "Just let us do all the hard work."

"Consider this your payment for all the free babysitting I've done over the past ten years," Ty said, and turned for the stairs.

"Damn. Can't even argue that." Matt said behind him.

"Fucker."

Ty snorted as he went back outside to unload more boxes from the U-Haul. Thank God the weather had cooperated. He understood now why nobody moved in winter. You never knew if it was going to hail or snow or be ball-chillingly cold. Luckily, it was none of them today, the temperature only minus five with no wind chill to speak of.

"Where do you want this box?" his sister asked.

He checked the side of the box—*bedsheets*, he'd written in marker—and sent Jenn to the upstairs hall closet. He was heading into the house with a couple of suitcases full of clothes when Maddie passed him on her way out.

"Dad's upstairs assembling your bed," she said, "and Mom's putting the cutlery in a drawer above the garbage can." Her face told him what she thought of that idea.

"That's disgusting," Ty said.

"I figured you were letting her do whatever she wanted with the kitchen, and then you'll go in there and change everything around once we leave."

Exactly. There was no use arguing about what went where when he could move it to where he wanted after everyone was gone. His mother had very specific *ideas* about where things should be placed in a kitchen—something to do with energies and flow and windows and nothing to do with practicality. The fact that it was *his* kitchen and that *he* should have the final say about where everything went made no difference to her.

"Smart girl," he said to Maddie. She grinned at him, braces catching the light, and trounced down the crushed stone driveway to the truck.

Maddie was the youngest after him. They got along the best despite the nine years between them, probably because their older siblings had dubbed them the "Accident Babies" since the day they were born. Ty was seven years younger than Jenn, which meant he was nine years younger than Jeremy and Matt.

He and Maddie had always been a team. She was the only one he would miss not seeing every day.

"Dude, the seventies threw up on your kitchen," Matt said on his way out the door.

Ty had to laugh. Because the seventies *had* thrown up on his kitchen. He'd had a week to paint the bedrooms, the hallways, and the dining room. He could've done the kitchen, too, but the more time he spent there, the more he started to like the turquoise cupboards and green-and-white walls.

"Hey, Dad," Ty said, depositing his suitcases in a corner of his new bedroom. "You didn't have to put my bed together."

"Are you kidding?" Marty Green said around the screws between his lips. He slotted them into the headboard and twisted everything into place. "Let your brothers do the heavy lifting. Old guy like me with a bad back? I'll stick to the easy stuff."

At sixty-years old, his dad liked to joke that he was old, but he didn't look a day past fifty.

"Tyler." His mom stood in the doorway. "You don't have a KitchenAid mixer."

"Well, I don't bake, so..." He left the rest of that obvious sentence hanging.

Sue Green nodded decisively. "I'll pick one up for you next time I'm at the store," she said, and headed back down to the kitchen.

Ty's exasperated eyes met his dad's amused ones. "Why do I even bother?"

"I don't know," his dad said. "She'll do whatever she wants regardless of what anyone says. You know that."

Ty helped his dad put the rest of the bed together then stood to survey the room.

"Should I have taken the master downstairs?"

His dad gave him a guileless look. "But this one has the window seat." He sounded like a kid, an overgrown one who knew his fourth child extremely well. Window seat trumped patio doors.

"Hi." A throat being cleared from the direction of the doorway. "The teenager outside told me to come up."

"Elias!" Whoa! *Tamp down the excitement, there, boyo.* "You made it," Ty said a little more sedately.

Man, even dressed down in pressed dark jeans and a deep purple polo, Elias looked like he was heading into the office for a business meeting. Neat beard, gelled hair, he looked ready to fire a person or seven.

Abominable job aside, Elias was a nice guy, if quiet and a bit hard to get to know. On top of their impromptu coffee date on Thursday morning, they'd gotten together on Friday morning as well. Elias had purposely—at least Ty liked to think so—sought him out on Friday morning to ask him out for coffee again. It was a nice break from Ty's usual everyday routine, and he got the impression that Elias needed the break from office life, too, despite the bid for the open VP position he'd said he was gunning for.

"Sorry I'm late," Elias said. "Took me longer than I thought to get here. I didn't realize you were moving so far out of the city."

"Hi there." His dad held out a hand to Elias. "I'm Marty, Ty's dad."

"Elias. It's good to meet you, sir."

"Elias is a friend of mine," Ty told his dad. "He offered to help me move today."

"That's really nice of you," his dad said, packing away his tools. "How do you two know each other?"

"We work in the same neighbourhood."

Elias raised an eyebrow at Ty's answer. *What? You don't want to tell your dad how you got mad at me for putting my newspaper in the wrong trash can?*

Ty was happy to tell his dad anything Elias wanted. His dad would just tell him that was typical Ty behaviour. He grinned at Elias. *Sure, but then I'd have to tell him that you bribed me with hot drinks and an apple turnover for three days.*

Elias seemed to get the message. His cheeks reddened.

On such a strikingly handsome and confident man, the blushing was rather adorable. Ty stood there like a tool, just smiling at Elias until Elias's blush reached his ears. Elias cleared his throat again and looked away.

"How can I help?" he asked. "The U-Haul was empty when I drove up. Sorry I didn't get here in time to help unload."

Ty's dad waved his apology away. "Don't worry about that. My oldest boys had it covered. Ty, your curtains are over there." He gestured to the window seat. "Maybe Elias could help you put those up?" He was out the door a second later, tool box in one hand.

"I can do those on my own later," Ty said. "Wanna help me set up the TV downstairs?"

Brushing past Elias, the tiny hairs on Ty's arms stood straight at attention when their arms touched. He got a whiff of Elias's cologne: spices and wood. God, why did Elias have to smell so good on top of looking so good? Ty had to stop himself from lunging at him. He wanted that scent all over him, in every pore until he was smelling it for weeks. The best way he could think of to do that would be to get them both naked and sharing the same small, enclosed space. Like underneath his bed covers.

His sisters and mother arguing in the kitchen successfully halted any boner that might've developed. Family was good for that.

"That flower pot goes on top of the fridge, Maddison."

"But Ty said he wanted it on the windowsill above the sink so it gets lots of light."

"Fridge, Maddison."

"But it'll die up there."

"Fridge."

"And then he'll cry big, fat, sad tears because his favourite plant is dead."

Ty chuckled quietly at Maddie's fib. He couldn't see his family from where he and Elias stood in front of the basement stairs, but he could hear them plenty well.

"Good, then maybe he'll think twice about moving all the way out here and come back home where he belongs until he gets married."

"Your antiquated ways are showing again, Mom," Jenn piped in.

"Maddie, you should head to Vegas and marry the first man you meet." That was Matt.

"Yeah, then we'd really see Mom blow a gasket." Jeremy finished Matt's thought, setting them both laughing.

"Why do my children think they're hilarious? Jeremy, stop pretending to fornicate with the spatula. Matthew, stop laughing. Jennifer, you're putting the mugs in the wrong cupboard."

"No, I'm not. Ty's got a sticky right here. Says *mugs*."

"He's got it all wrong. Plates need to go in there. The mugs are going over here. Maddison. Flower pot. Fridge. Where's your father?"

Probably staying far away, if he had any sense.

Half amused, half embarrassed, Ty turned to Elias, ready to make a joke, but Elias looked slightly overwhelmed by the commotion, so Ty led him downstairs instead.

I know you like things in their proper place, Capricorn, but you can't always get your way.

TY CROWED WHEN NETFLIX WORKED ON THE SMART TV they mounted onto the wall. Meant the internet was properly hooked up. Out here in Boontown, you never knew.

Elias sat on the ugly blue and pink couch and watched Ty adjust the screen resolution on his TV. The couch was so old and so low to the ground that it swallowed Elias in despite his five-foot-ten height, cupping around him like a bowl, preventing him from getting up.

Good thing he had no interest in going anywhere. Sitting here eyeing Ty's perfectly round ass was enough for him.

Ty's new house was miniature, with narrow hallways and small bedrooms. Granted it was bigger than his own condo downtown, where the cars passing by on the Gardiner Expressway below made it too loud to use the balcony he'd paid extra for. Ty's house had a cool seventies vibe to it, which somehow suited Ty perfectly.

To be honest, Elias was a little jealous of this charming house and the land it sat on. It was peaceful and quiet, far from the hype of downtown Toronto, no nearby neighbours, no highway sounds, no smell of cigarette smoke and sewer water. He spent approximately two seconds weighing the pros and cons of moving out here himself, but one con outweighed all the pros: it would take him two and a half hours in rush-hour traffic to drive to and from his office in the downtown core. Each way. Ty was lucky—he worked six to two, so it would take him an hour, hour and a half, tops.

Half of Ty's basement was finished. The other half was a storage area. The finished area was a cozy den. It was also about ten degrees colder than the rest of the house, but Ty had thought ahead and brought down a half dozen throws.

Ty finally fixed the resolution on the TV the way he wanted it, and the settings screen disappeared, leaving the Netflix home screen in its stead.

Continue watching for Ty, Elias read. Curious as to what Ty liked to watch, he glanced at the list. *Quantico*, *Flipped*—whatever that was—*Star Trek: Voyager*, *Digimon*, *Stranger Things*, and—

Elias sat up—or tried to on the stupid couch. "You like *Legend of Korra*?"

Ty turned to him, eyebrows raised in surprise. "*You* like *Legend of Korra*?"

Why did he say that like the thought was impossible to grasp?

"Team Mako or Team Asami?" Ty asked. The look on his face told Elias he didn't expect him to know what he was talking about.

Elias scoffed. "Asami. Mako's a moron."

"He has a cool power, though," Ty said. He sat on the couch, getting swallowed up by the monstrosity on his end. Wedged into the corner made by the arm and back, his legs sprawled in front of him, wearing baggy jeans and a loose T-shirt, he didn't look a day over the eighteen years Elias had first thought him to be. Elias looked thirty-two, he knew that, and lusting after an eighteen-year-old lookalike made him feel old and pervy.

"Korra's is better," he said. "She can do everything."

"I don't know, man," Ty disagreed. "Mako's lightning, and the way he uses it in the series finale? That was awesome."

"Yeah, but Korra—"

"Ty, I put your curtains up," Mr. Green said, coming into the basement.

"Thanks, Dad. You didn't have to."

Mr. Green grunted. "Kept me out of the kitchen." He sat in the huge armchair that matched the couch. If the couch swallowed both Elias and Ty, the armchair looked like it'd suck in any unwilling body like a vacuum and never let them go. "You put the TV up but didn't bother with your bedroom curtains, I see."

"Thought if I stayed down here, Mom wouldn't find me."

"Maddison, that box doesn't go in the basement."

Elias stiffened at what he assumed was Mrs. Green's voice coming from the top of the basement stairs.

"Yes, it does." The voice belonged to the teenager who'd told Elias to head upstairs when he'd first arrived. "See? Ty wrote it right here on the box."

"Let me see that." The sound of a box being opened, contents shuffling. "These don't belong in the basement. Put them in the spare bedroom."

It took everything Elias had not march over to the stairs, take the box from Maddison, and deposit it right here, in the basement, where Ty wanted it. On the other end of the couch, Ty simply rolled his eyes. How could he just sit there and let his mother dictate what should go where in his own house? Elias would be livid. In fact, he *was* livid on Ty's behalf. He had to force the words that wanted to come out back down his throat so he didn't say anything mean.

Next to him Ty took a piece of paper and a small pencil out of his pocket and wrote a line at the bottom of what appeared to be a list.

An avalanche of feet coming down the basement stairs distracted them both. A tall set of blond twins appeared.

"Dude, one of your boxes marked *basement* ended up in the second bedroom upstairs," one of them said.

"Yeah, I know," Ty said. "I heard. I've got it written." He waved the list in his hand.

"Ty," another blonde said, this one female, but not the teenager he'd met earlier. "I tried to organize as much as I could in the kitchen based on your directions, but—" she plopped down on the couch between them "—Mom caught me a few times, so you'll need to do some reorganizing. Sorry."

"Hey, Ty, we're leaving soon." *There* was the blonde teenager. Jesus, how many siblings did Ty have? "Mom's just packing up the rest of the sandwiches for you."

"Take the tuna with you," Ty instructed. "I don't like tuna."

"I'll eat them," Elias said, which had every blond head in the room swinging his way as if they'd only now noticed his presence. Given he was the only brown guy in the room, it was slightly hysterical.

"Hi." The woman next to him held out a hand and shot him a smile identical to Ty's. "I'm Jenn."

"Guys," Ty said. "This is my friend Elias. Elias, these are

my brothers and sisters: the twins, Matt and Jeremy. That's Jenn, and this is Maddie."

There was that dreaded word again. *Friend*. Elias had been friend-zoned already. How did he get himself out of it? Hell, how had he gotten himself *into* it in the first place? He wanted to date Ty, not be his friend. Although he'd take friendship if that was all Ty was willing to give him.

Fuck, dating was complicated. No wonder he avoided it.

Everyone acknowledged him briefly...then ignored him, which had the breath Elias was holding whooshing from his nose in one shot. The fact that he didn't have to sit here talking about himself, being scrutinized by all the Green kids, had him relaxing back into his own corner of the couch.

And since no one was paying attention to him, he took a few minutes to answer a couple of important emails on his phone while everyone else talked around him as if he didn't exist.

"Ty, give me the keys to the U-Haul," one of the twins said. "Matt and I will drop it off on the way back to the city."

"It's got to be back by six." Ty fished the keys out of his pocket and handed them to his brother. "Otherwise I'll get charged extra. Is that enough time?"

"If we leave now."

"All right, everybody." And there was Major General Mom, casually strolling into the basement as if she owned it, not her son. "Time to head out. Ty, everything in the kitchen's been unpacked. Everything else is up to you."

"Thanks, Mom," Ty said.

"I left you a grocery list on your counter. The only things you have right now are the few sandwiches we didn't eat, bottled water, and a box of Shreddies."

She kept talking, instructing Ty on what he needed to buy to stock his kitchen. Elias tuned her out, and so did the Green siblings, if the way they spoke to each other behind her back using their own made-up version of sign language was any indication.

"Oh!"

Elias looked up to find her gaze—sepia-coloured, unlike the ice blue of her husband and kids—on him.

"Hello, there."

After Ty made quick introductions, Elias held out a hand. "Nice to meet you, Mrs. Green," he lied. She was a steam-roller, and she had all of his defences up.

"A friend, Ty said?" Mrs. Green asked. "Are you coming to his birthday party next Saturday?"

Ty groaned. "Mom, I'm turning *twenty*-seven not *seven*. I don't need parties anymore."

She merely raised a dark eyebrow at her son. "Be there by two." She pointed at everyone except Ty and Elias. "Let's get going." And disappeared upstairs.

Maddie patted Ty's arm. "Don't worry. I'll make your favourite cake."

Ty whimpered. "With the triple layer of icing? I love you."

The Green clan was gone five minutes later. Elias hovered in the entranceway as Ty said goodbye to his family. Was he supposed to leave, too? The only thing he'd done so far was help Ty mount the TV in the basement. He'd offered to help Ty move in—mostly to get out of the blind-date Rachel had set up between him and her cousin—but he hadn't really done anything. It had taken him much longer to get out of the city than he'd thought, and he'd shown up late, after all the hard stuff was already done.

Ty shut the door on the last of his family and leaned back against it. Smile a mile wide, he looked happy and young and carefree.

"Finally alone," he said.

Elias didn't know if he meant "finally alone" like, "I'm finally alone in my own house." Or "finally alone" like, "We're finally alone, just the two of us. Let's go have sex now!" Either way, it made Elias think of the king-sized bed he'd seen upstairs, and he enjoyed a brief fantasy of christening the new house by fucking Ty blind on it.

But then he remembered how crappy he'd felt after his last one-night stand. He didn't want Ty to be a one-night stand or a casual fling. So instead he said, "How can I help?"

Ty pursed his pink, full lips—Elias had to force his eyes up—and seemed to think about it.

"How do you feel about organizing?"

Chapter Four

Elias, it turned out, loved to organize.

Problem was, so did Ty. Which meant they disagreed on where everything should go in the kitchen.

"Why would you put the pans in the cupboard furthest away from the stove?" Elias asked, eyeing the distance between said cupboard and stove. "You use pans *on* the stove. Thus, the pans should be close to the stove."

He had a point there. Ty wasn't such a stick-in-the-mud that he couldn't admit to being wrong, and putting the pans closer to the stove *was* a good idea. So, he took Elias's suggestion and made a few swaps.

"Your notes say you're planning on putting your spices in the pantry." Elias squinted at the digital notepad on Ty's phone.

"Yeah, so?"

"Spices go on a spice rack," Elias instructed. "And the spice rack sits on the counter next to the stove, since that's where the cooking happens."

Clearly Elias—just like Ty's mom—had ideas about where things should go in a kitchen. But unlike his mom, if Ty explained why he wanted things the way he did, Elias actually listened and even often agreed with Ty's well-thought-out argument.

"Well, the point is moot right now, anyway," Ty said, addressing Elias's point about the spices. "Because I don't have a spice rack or spices." His mom wasn't kidding when she said all he had to eat was a box of cereal, the leftover sandwiches from the day's lunch, and water. So, they ordered a pizza.

It arrived forty minutes later, and they pounced on it like starving animals. Instead of working while they ate, they brought the entire pie down to the basement along with some water bottles and watched *Legend of Korra* on Netflix.

He still couldn't believe Elias was a fan. He was so straight-laced, he seemed more like a *West Wing* fan or *Law & Order* or *Suits* or *How to Get Away With Murder*. But Elias laughed at all the good parts, especially at the opening scene where Korra told everyone that she was the avatar and they'd have to deal with it. And in episode five when a lovesick Bolin burst into pathetic tears at the sight of Korra and Mako kissing. And he laughed his ass off at the antics of Tenzin's kids, who, Ty had to admit, stole every scene they were in.

Turned out, it was way more fun watching Elias watch the show than it was watching the show itself. Ty kept one eye on the TV and one on Elias, so he could watch Elias's reactions while the other man was unaware. Ty had watched *Korra* enough times that he could repeat entire dialogues verbatim. Elias watched it like it was his first time.

It was nice to see Elias relaxed for the first time all day. He'd been tense since he arrived, whether because he didn't like large crowds, or because he was uncomfortable around people he didn't know, or because he regretted his offer to help, it was hard to tell. He'd looked both a little irritated and a lot relieved when Ty's family hadn't spent more than four seconds acknowledging his presence earlier. The best Ty could figure was that Elias was like him—he liked to be acknowledged, but he didn't want to be the centre of attention.

Elias grinned when the Fire Ferrets won the pro-bending championship on *Korra*. That killer smile of his was a kick to Ty's solar plexus. Normally Ty had no idea what

Elias was thinking at any given moment. He was so serious, rarely smiled. But unguarded like this, he was much easier to read. Ty had found Elias staring at him off and on—mostly on—all day. Sometimes as if Ty was a complicated puzzle he was trying to solve. Other times as if he wanted to pet him.

Ty would be so, so good with the petting, but oftentimes he thought he might be imagining that look on Elias's face. And because he was so hard to read, Ty had no idea if the man was actually interested in him or not.

They ended up watching the first ten episodes of season one. At twenty-three minutes per episode, it meant he lost almost four hours of unpacking, but whatever. He had the next week off to do exactly that. For now, he enjoyed sitting next to and getting to know Elias. How often did he have a chance to sit companionably beside a hot guy he was into without his parents or one of his siblings hanging around?

God, it was good to be out of his parents' house. He still couldn't believe this house was all his.

It was after ten by the time Elias started making noises about heading home.

"How long do you think it'll take me to get home at this time of night?" Elias asked as he crouched to tie his boot laces in Ty's front entranceway.

"Probably only an hour or so, if you don't hit any traffic." One would think there'd be no traffic at ten o'clock on a Saturday evening, but in the GTA, you never knew. Given that the clubs were just staring to get going downtown Toronto, he might run into a whole bunch of suburbanites heading into the city to party.

"That'd be a nice change." Elias stood and took his coat out of the front hall closet. "Took me two and a half hours to get here."

Ty winced. He felt bad for not telling Elias how far out of

the city he'd moved, so he made an offer that was probably not the wisest but would hopefully tell him where he stood.

"You could, uh..." He faltered briefly under Elias's liquid brown gaze. "You could stay the night? Head home in the morning?"

Those eyes went molten in an instant, leaving no guesses as to how Elias felt about Ty. It made Ty's breath catch and his mouth went dry. He took an instinctive step forward into Elias's personal space. From what Ty had been able to tell over the past few days, the man had a pretty big personal space bubble; Ty fully expected him to pull back. Instead, Elias met him halfway, settling his hands on Ty's waist.

"I don't think that's a good idea," Elias said, so softly it was almost a whisper. "Not yet anyway."

Ty's breath left him in a disappointed whoosh. "Yeah, you're probably right."

Heart kicking his ribs, he stared into Elias's eyes, only an inch or so above his own. Elias looked as unwilling to leave as Ty was unwilling to let him go.

Elias licked his lips—Ty watched that tongue, dying for a taste—squeezed Ty's waist, and took a step back. "I'll see you on Monday morning?" he asked, voice gone deeper than normal.

"Actually..." Ty had to swallow past the want in his throat. "I took the week off, so I could get settled here."

"Oh."

Elias looked as disappointed as Ty felt.

"So, I'll see you...next Monday, then?" Elias asked.

"Yeah."

Elias brushed his thumb against Ty's cheek, and Ty had to hold in a whimper of need at that one brief contact that left him wanting so much more.

Elias was out the door a second later.

Ty groaned and rested his forehead against the door's

frosted glass window. He didn't want to wait until next Monday to see Elias. He wanted to see him again right *now*.

A knock on the door. He opened it to reveal a scowling Elias.

Wow. Wishes really did come true.

"It's not because I don't want to," Elias growled, looking both turned on and sexily annoyed. "I just don't think we should rush things."

Ty nodded. He wasn't a jump-into-bed type of guy either. But he didn't have to like it. "I get it," he whispered.

Elias let out a purring growl, and before Ty had finished shivering at the sound, Elias was once again in the house, pressing Ty's back up against the wall next to the closet door, mouth on his.

The whine Ty let loose as his lips were hotly overtaken was desperate and aroused but he didn't care. Tongues tangling and fighting for dominance, neither one of them gave in, settling into a kiss made of want and ferocity that had them both panting.

Ty loved it. Loved that Elias wasn't careful with him. Simply took what he wanted, no apology.

Elias tasted like he smelled, spices and wood. Ty licked into his mouth again, grabbing every taste of Elias's desire that he could. Elias's body pressed his firmly against the wall, and Ty could feel every inch of him...including what felt like an incredible eight-inch boner in his pants.

Pulling away to gasp in a much-needed breath, they stood forehead to forehead, breathing hard. But Ty wanted more, and he wanted it now. Palming the back of Elias's head, he brought his mouth back down to his. Elias's beard rasped against his chin, scraped his face.

He revelled in it, the prickles against his skin ramping up his need.

Elias's thumb pressed against Ty's chin, encouraging him

to open wider. His other hand squeezed Ty's ass, grinding their erections together. They lost time as they made out against the wall, rutting against each other. Elias had shed his jacket at some point—Ty didn't even remember when, just knew that he'd gone from gripping the back of Elias's jacket to gripping his T-shirt. Then his hands were finding their way underneath said T-shirt to spread over Elias's strong, smooth back.

God, oh fuckity, fuck, he needed to come, had to come, right now, and the friction of their dicks rubbing against each other through their jeans simply wasn't enough. Elias must've read his mind—or his body, as it were. He took a single step back, unzipped them both, and had both their hard dicks in one hand a second later.

Ty's head thunked against the wall behind him, eyes clenched shut, the feel of their bare erections together in Elias's hand too much and yet not enough. "Oh, God, oh, fuck, Eli," he sobbed. Forcing his eyes open, he looked down, because God, did he want to see.

Ty was right about Elias's eight inches. His brown cock nestled next to Ty's pale one in Elias's tight fist was enough to have pre-come leaking out of his tip. Elias's dick wasn't only darker and longer than Ty's but wider as well. Ty wanted it in his mouth so badly he had to swallow past the saliva buildup, but he didn't want to move too much in case Elias came to his senses and changed his mind about this.

"Yes," Elias whispered, using a thumb to rub Ty's pre-come along both their lengths, making it easier for him to slide his hand up and down. "Fuck, that's hot."

"I gotta come," Ty whined.

"I know, baby," Elias said, voice heavy. For some reason the endearment had little butterflies fluttering in Ty's stomach. "Gonna come for me now?"

"Fuck, yes. Eli, harder."

Elias took him at his word, tightening his grasp to the point of pain. Grabbing Elias's T-shirt, he brought him forward until their mouths were again locked together. Elias's free hand wound its way down the back of Ty's boxers—which were still half on his ass—his fingers lightly playing at Ty's taint.

Ty tore his mouth away from Elias's. "Fuck, Eli."

"Gonna come?" Elias asked again, the words sounding torn from his throat. Sweat dripped off them both, Elias's pre-come mixing with Ty's.

"Yes. Please. Harder."

Elias buried his face in Ty's neck, biting the sensitive skin between Ty's shoulder and neck at the same time that he once again tightened his hand on their dicks.

Ty lost it. One hand yanking on Elias's hair, nails of the other digging into Elias's broad back, Ty bucked as fire took over his body and came all over Elias's fist.

Elias was right behind, growling Ty's name into his neck.

They stood there, slumped against the wall for a few minutes, trying to get their breathing under control until Elias lifted his head and said, "Yes," with a wrung-out voice that sounded like it came from the bottom of his reserves.

"Yes, what?"

"Yes, I'll stay the night."

Chapter Five

AN ORGASM, AS IT TURNED OUT, MADE TY SLEEPY. OR IT was possible he was tired from the move. Either way, he passed out, cuddled against Elias, almost as soon as Elias returned from cleaning himself up and using his finger and a bit of Ty's toothpaste in the bathroom to clean his teeth.

Snuggled together in Ty's big bed, the cuddling told Elias this wasn't a one-time thing for Ty, and that made him feel a whole lot better about breaking his own rules. Actually, more like *rule*—singular. Namely to wait before jumping into bed with Ty, so they could get to know each other better. Ty had seemed to be on the same page.

Too bad their libidos had other ideas. Oh well. No use dwelling on it. The deed was done, so to speak. It was the first time Elias had engaged in sexual activity of any kind and not felt awful afterward. He'd like to think that was because this wasn't a one-night stand. Ty's quick blindingly joyful smile when Elias had said he would stay the night was proof he was as invested as Elias himself.

He dreamed of sex with Ty, of Ty tonguing him, licking up his length then back down until he reached Elias's testicles. Pulling one into his mouth with his tongue, sucking hard, he used his hand to squeeze Elias's shaft.

"Fuck yes, suck me," he said in the dream.

Ty obeyed. Abandoning his balls, he played with the tip of Elias's cock, licking underneath the rim, tonguing his slit. Hand massaging the skin between his balls, Ty bent forward and sucked him all the way in.

Elias groaned loudly. Everything tightened, preparing to

bust apart, heat lapping down his spine, curling his toes into the mattress. Ty hummed, and Elias woke up coming down Ty's throat, hands fisted in the sheets, screaming Ty's name.

Ty cleaned him up with his tongue as Elias lay there, blinking dumbly into the bright Sunday morning sunshine, utterly spent yet invigorated at the same time. Ty kissed his way up Elias's body, paying close attention to his nipples then sucking gently on the skin of his neck. Elias ran his hand through Ty's soft hair and brought his head up so he could look at him.

"Hi," Ty said, smiling. His hair was plastered to his head on one side and sticking straight up on the other. It made him look even more like the eighteen-year-old Elias kept thinking him to be. The morning stubble, however, bumped him up to, oh, about twenty-one.

He should keep the stubble.

"Hi," Elias said, smiling back at him. He cleared the sleep and sex out of his voice. "Can you wake me up like that every morning before I go to work?"

Ty laughed and pecked him quickly on the lips. "I start work three hours before you," he pointed out, straddling Elias's stomach. "So really it would be *you* waking *me* up before work."

Elias took in Ty's muscled torso, the sleep creases on his shoulder, the pink nipples, the tapered waist. His treasure trail was a darker blond than the hair on his head, and it arrowed straight down into curly pubes and a painful looking erection.

"Gonna fuck me with that?" he asked.

"Can I?" Ty asked, eyebrows winging up to his hairline, clearly surprised that Elias enjoyed being fucked as much as he enjoyed doing the fucking, but then Ty's shoulders slumped. "But I couldn't find the condoms. Or lube." He looked mournfully at something in the corner of the room.

Elias followed his gaze to where a couple of boxes marked *bathroom* sat open next to the door.

Hmm, no condoms? No lube? That was fine. They were gay men. There were workarounds.

"Get up here, then," he said. "Fuck my mouth."

Red spots stole over Ty's cheeks when he was really turned on—like last night—and they did so again now. Ty swore softly and readjusted himself over Elias's chest, legs splayed wide on either side of him. Elias opened up, letting Ty feed him his cock. Batting Ty's hand away, Elias grasped the base of Ty's dick and tongued the tip, giving him a proper tongue bath that had Ty sucking in a harsh breath through his teeth.

Elias took him in, using a bit of teeth as well as tongue and lips. Judging by yesterday, Ty appeared to enjoy a bit of pain with his orgasm. Elias bit down—very, *very* gently—and it was enough for Ty to fall forward, forehead landing on the arm braced along the top of the headboard.

"Mother...fucking...shit," Ty gritted out through a clenched jaw.

In this position, Ty's face was directly above Elias's. A muscle worked in Ty's jaw; his eyes squeezed shut. Inserting a finger into his own mouth next to Ty's salty dick, Elias got it good and wet before sneaking it behind Ty and fingering his ring. Once the muscles relaxed under his ministrations, he inserted his finger in one go and sucked hard on Ty's dick at the same time.

Ty shook uncontrollably, so hard Elias thought he might hurt himself.

"Eli," Ty said through a groan, thighs shaking against Elias's chest, hand fisted in the pillow by Elias's head. Above him Ty's eyes opened, ice blue desperately searching for something. "I need..."

Yeah, Elias knew what he needed.

Crooking the finger swallowed by Ty's hole, he found Ty's prostate and massaged it, letting his teeth come out to play on Ty's dick again. A flush stole up Ty's chest, and he came in Elias's mouth, come hitting the back of Elias's throat. Elias swallowed reflexively, Ty trembling around him, babbling incoherently.

"Fuck, Eli. God, I'm coming. I'm coming. Eli, fuuuuuuck, ungh..."

Ty was still shaking long seconds after he finished exploding in Elias's mouth. Elias gently removed his finger then licked Ty's dick clean before letting it fall out of his mouth. The soft cock landed on his cheek. Ty didn't seem capable of moving, so Elias ran his hands up and down his thighs, soothing him back down.

"Ty? Baby?"

Ty swallowed hard.

"You all right?"

He was *still* shaking as he shifted off Elias and flopped sideways next to him. "Never...better." Even his voice shook.

He was asleep thirty seconds later.

TWO HOURS LATER, THEY HIT FIRST A CHAIN GROCERY store in Guelph—Ty didn't even have milk to go with his one cereal box—then a small café where they had a late brunch.

"Did you know a banana is actually a berry?" Ty asked, apropos of nothing. "Says so right here." He slid his paper placemat—full of random food facts and pictures—closer to Elias. Elias's placemat had a fill-in-the-dots drawing, a tiny crossword, a word scrambler, a maze, and a spot-the-difference challenge.

"So, it's really a bananaberry?" Elias asked.

For some reason Ty thought that was hilarious.

After dropping the groceries off at Ty's, they headed to the Starkey Hill Interpretive Trail for some snowshoeing. Of course, it took Ty all of five seconds to find his snowshoes and poles, and yet the lube and condoms were still MIA.

But that was fine. They'd stocked up at the store.

Elias brought his camera. It went everywhere with him anyway, but he'd been an idiot yesterday, leaving it in his car all day and then overnight in the cold. He was damn lucky it had turned on this morning.

Landscape and wildlife photography were his passions, but he found himself distracted today by Ty's perfect face. Even in his ugly, poofy snowman coat he looked good enough to pounce on. He was a graceful angel on his snowshoes. By contrast Elias felt like an unbalanced bear. He kept forgetting to widen his stance so that he didn't step on his snowshoe frame with the other foot.

"What are you doing?"

Elias was on his back in the snow, camera held up to his face as he focused on a blue jay in a leafless tree above him. From below like this, it'd be a really cool shot, the bird's blue feathers stark against the dull brown tree branches. He could submit the photo to *CanadaBirds*—a sister magazine of *CanadaTravels*—for consideration. Zooming his lens accordingly and adjusting his manual settings, he tried to keep very still so the bird didn't get scared and take off. He wanted a bit of a blurry background so he set his f-stop to—

—A nose pinked from the cold appeared in his viewfinder. He was so surprised he hit the shutter-release by accident. And when he saw the image that appeared on his monitor, he couldn't help but chuckle, sending the blue jay scurrying off.

"What's so funny?"

Elias turned the camera to show Ty. Ty peered at it, squinted, and said, "I look hot."

It was a picture of his left nostril and part of his eye.

Elias kept laughing.

"Here, take a better one," Ty said and plopped down in the snow next to Elias.

"Oh, no," Elias said. "I don't really get in front of the cam—"

Ty had the picture taken before Elias could finish his sentence. Except none of the settings had been adjusted, so instead of a selfie of the two of them, Elias had a blurry picture of what might have been his own beard or maybe the tree trunk behind them.

Ty cracked up.

Elias took a picture of him like that, head thrown back, eyes half-closed, mouth wide, teeth glistening bright as the snow that had gotten into his hair. That way he'd have this moment forever and could always look back on it and remember how good it felt to be in that honeymoon phase of dating someone who felt about Elias the same way Elias felt about him, when everything was wonderful and new and fun.

That carefree laughter was the best kind of kick in the gut. Without thinking twice about it, he moved in on Ty and kissed his still laughing mouth. Ty was still chuckling as he kissed Elias back, mouth cold, tongue warm. It took hardly any prompting from Elias for Ty to roll himself on top of him but Ty's coat was so slick that he landed on Elias and then slipped off him, landing on Elias's other side, which only made him laugh harder. His good mood was contagious, and Elias laughed with him until the snow started soaking into his jeans.

"Come on, you goof," Elias said, getting up with difficulty. Stupid snowshoes. "Let's head back so we can get out of this cold."

The wind chill was supposed to drop again overnight, and they could already feel it even though sunset was still three hours away.

"Let's go winter camping," Ty said, standing much more nimbly.

"What, *now*?"

Never happen.

"No, not now." Ty headed back onto the trail. Elias followed. "Next weekend?"

"You have a birthday party next weekend," Elias reminded him, eyes on his feet so he didn't trip himself up again. "Plus," he continued, so that Ty didn't think he was angling for an invite, "I hate to break it to you...but I don't camp in winter."

"Awww, but I wanna go camping with you."

"Well, I wanna fuck you silly, so let's go do that instead."

For the first time since they started snowshoeing an hour and a half ago, Ty fell flat on his face.

***

It was Elias's fault entirely that the shower curtain ripped. Had the man not insisted that he needed to shower the day off him before they fell into bed, then Ty never would've followed him in there, lube and condom in hand.

Chest-to-chest with Elias's hard body, hot water raining onto his back, steam billowing around them, Ty felt safely protected in a cocoon of warmth. Elias's mouth on his tasted so good, like the cinnamon apples he'd eaten as part of his brunch today. His hands were everywhere on Ty's body as they kissed, licking into each other's mouths without hurry.

"You're so warm," Ty mumbled when Elias switched to kissing his neck. Ty ran his hands down Elias's back and pressed himself closer, craving Elias's heat.

"We *are* in a warm shower," Elias pointed out between kisses.

"Screw that logic. You're always warm."

Elias snorted, but it was true. He gave off heat. It was incredible.

Elias made his way down Ty's body, kissing and licking away the water droplets, driving Ty crazy in the process. Ty locked his thighs so he didn't fall, stomach clenching. He was drunk on lust, high on Elias. When Elias finally swallowed his dick, Ty hung on to the shower curtain for balance.

Elias looked up at him, eyes wicked, his hand following the path his mouth took. He gave a savage twist at the tip, making Ty squeeze his eyes shut in pleasure and pain. Elias sucked him in again, all the way to the back of his throat, and Ty's every thought left him, travelling down his spine and into his hard-on.

Elias gave one last suck and pulled off. "Turn around."

No, God, Ty needed to come right now.

"I know." Elias kept pumping his hand. Crap, had Ty said that out loud? "But I want to be in you when you do."

Elias released him, and Ty turned on shaky legs. He hung on to the shower curtain with one hand and braced the other on the wall in front of him, opening himself up to Elias. Elias ran his hands from Ty's shoulders, down his sides, ending on his ass where he pulled the cheeks apart.

"God, you're gorgeous," Elias said. Ty barely heard him over the sound of the water hitting the tub.

"Just fuck me already," Ty said. He could barely breathe with how much he wanted this.

There was the crinkle of the condom wrapper and then the *snick* of the tube of lube being opened. *Yes, finally!* Fuck, he couldn't wait to have Elias inside him for the first time. But instead of Elias's cock, it was Elias's finger pressing at his entrance and then through it, gliding in without resistance. Ty lifted his foot and rested it against the lip of the tub, giving Elias easier access.

"Fuck," Elias growled. "I'm not going to last once I get in you."

"Trust me," Ty said through a throat gone dry. "You won't be the only one who finishes fast."

A second finger joined the first in Ty's ass. His entire body went taut, and he tried not to come too soon. Spread out like this, he felt sinful and wicked. And when Elias bit his butt cheek at the same time that he scissored his fingers, Ty cried out and bucked back against Elias's hand, fire blazing down his spine.

Elias removed his fingers and squeezed the base of Ty's shaft, staving off his impending orgasm. Ty whimpered at the loss of stimulation.

"I hate you," he said, voice rough.

"Do you?" Elias said before the tip of his cock breached Ty's hole, rendering Ty mute and incoherent. The feel of Elias pushing his way inside him was both good and bad—good because Ty was desperate for him, and bad because Elias was purposely taking his goddamn time.

"You better fuck me hard," Ty demanded.

"Oh, I plan to," Elias said in Ty's ear once he was fully seated inside him, his front plastered against Ty's back. His breathing was just as harsh as Ty's. They stood still, getting used to each other. Every hard inch of Elias inside him was exquisite. Elias held him steady with one hand splayed across his abdomen. The other reached around and pinched his nipple.

"Ready?" Elias asked.

He didn't wait for an answer. And he didn't fuck Ty hard like he promised. He pumped his hips so agonizingly slowly that Ty thought he'd explode from frustrated desire. His knees went liquid, and then it was all he could do to keep himself upright when Elias slammed home and went to town, nailing his gland with every thrust.

"Yes, yes, yes," he chanted in time with each of Elias's thrusts. "Yes, yes, yes, Eli."

Ty grabbed his dick and squeezed...and he was done, body coming undone, shooting onto the wall in front of him while Elias continued to do him hard, the hot water showering down onto their heads. Behind him, Elias stiffened, growling in his ear as he came.

Breathing hard, Elias buried his face in Ty's neck, still holding onto Ty with that one hand on his stomach. For some reason it made Ty feel cherished and safe. He turned his head, seeking Elias's mouth. Apparently, Elias could read his mind: he lifted his head from Ty's neck and took Ty's lips with his own, the hunger in them doing nothing to settle Ty's racing heart.

The loud *rriipp* almost had Ty pitching sideways. Elias caught him before he could go down with the curtain, steadying them both in the slippery bathtub. He reached around Ty to turn the water off, preventing it from pooling onto the tiled bathroom floor.

"Shit," Elias said.

"Oops." Ty chuckled.

"You would think that's funny," Elias said.

How could it be anything but?

They spent a few minutes cleaning up—throwing away the destroyed curtain, mopping up the small puddle that had formed. Ty couldn't stop laughing the whole time, which made Elias smile at him indulgently.

Man, his guy was hot, squatting there naked, using a towel to soak up the water on the floor. Well-defined chest, hard thighs, that big dick dangling between his legs, and those arms...those arms had held Ty up when the curtain had fallen.

"You going to just stand there, or do you feel like helping?" Elias asked.

Ty cocked his head, gaze at Elias's nimble fingers turning

the towel around to use the dry side. Fingers that had recently been in Ty's body. He shivered.

"Don't rush or anything," Elias said, a slight smile on his face. "I'll just clean up your mess all by myself."

"*My* mess?" Ty raised his eyebrows, enjoying the game. "This is all your fault, you know."

"You were the one hanging on to the curtain," Elias pointed out.

"You were the one who fucked me so hard I couldn't see straight."

Elias's chest puffed out.

They fell into Ty's bed minutes later, the wet towels in the washer in the basement, the floor clean, and the useless curtain in a bag by the front door, ready to be taken out to the trash cans in the garage.

"I'll get you a new curtain," Elias said.

Ty snuggled closer and slung an arm around Elias's waist, letting his eyes fall closed. "Don't worry about it." He patted Elias's chest. "I'll go to the store later."

"Baby, you're not going anywhere."

"Am too."

"You're about to fall asleep."

"No," Ty said, and did just that.

TY WOKE UP ALONE TWENTY MINUTES LATER, READY TO have another go at Elias. But the smell coming from downstairs had him rifling through his still-unpacked suitcase for a pair of boxers and a hoodie and heading to the kitchen to find his missing man. Who, it turned out, was making grilled cheese in a buttered pan instead of using the electric grill like any other self-sufficient male adult.

Elias smiled at him over his shoulder. "Hey. Sorry for

invading your kitchen, but my stomach started making noises ten minutes ago."

"It's fine." Ty hugged him from behind and stood on tippy toes to peek over his shoulder. The bread was perfectly browned on both sides, and he was using cheese he'd sliced from the block of cheddar Ty had bought earlier instead of the individually wrapped slices he'd also bought.

"I was going to make pasta," Elias was saying, "but you don't have any canned tomatoes or tomato paste."

"I have a jar of pasta sauce in the pantry."

Elias's nose wrinkled.

"Ah," Ty said, stepping away. "I see."

"What do you see?"

Ty took a couple of plates out of the cupboard. "You're a food snob," he joked.

"What?" Elias looked briefly offended, but then he appeared to think about it. Finally, he shrugged. "Actually, you're probably right."

Ty laughed, loving that Elias was unapologetic about who he was and what he liked.

Since Ty didn't have any tables yet, they took their grilled cheeses and bottles of water to the basement, where they sat next to each other on the couch under a warm, fuzzy throw and watched an episode of *Legend of Korra* on Netflix while they ate.

"Hey," Ty said mid-episode when something occurred to him. "Can I see the pictures you took today?"

"Oh, um..." Elias fidgeted and looked away, picking at the crust of his sandwich.

"You don't have to—"

"No," Elias interrupted. "It's just that I actually didn't take that many."

Ty would've sworn he'd heard that *schwick* sound of the shutter button quite a few times today. Maybe Elias didn't like sharing his images with others. That was fine. Ty wasn't going to pry.

"How long have you been into photography?" he asked instead.

"A long time," Elias said, polishing off his meal. "I got a camera as a gift for my eighth birthday, a fake kid's one that didn't even take real pictures. You'd just point, shoot, and click, but it didn't produce an image. I've been taking pictures ever since."

"How come you don't do it professionally?"

Elias frowned. "That's not a real job."

"How so?"

"Establishing yourself as a photographer is hard, and there are so many out there that any one of them could come along at any time and snag your job away from you. There's no job security."

"That could be said of every job, though," Ty argued.

"Not really," Elias countered. "Take my job now, for example. I'm really good at it. If somebody better than me came along, I wouldn't automatically be replaced unless I sucked at my job. With photography it's different. You can be replaced even if you're great."

That was some fucked up logic, there. Ty didn't even know where to begin ripping that apart. And he didn't think Elias being good at his job of assessing organizational "reorganizations" was necessarily a good thing.

"How about you?" Elias asked. "What did you want to be when you were younger?"

"A vet," Ty said. "But then my brothers told me that sometimes it would mean having to euthanize animals and—" He gave a rueful smile. "—I changed my mind right quick."

"Do you ever think of going back to school?" Elias said. "Doing something else?"

"No. Why would I?"

"If you got your GED, you could go to college. It would open up a lot of opportunities for you." Elias took a sip out of his water bottle, as if the force of the words he'd so casually spoken hadn't slammed into Ty's chest like well-aimed bullets.

"What makes you think I don't have an education?"

Something in Ty's voice must've given him away, because Elias froze in the act of recapping his water bottle. He set the bottle on the floor by his foot and turned to Ty, brow furrowed.

"Am I wrong?" he asked, looking for all the world genuinely perplexed by the daggers Ty was sure were shooting out of his eyes.

"I graduated high school when I was eighteen," Ty said, voice tight. "I have a Bachelor of Science in biology from U of T and a post-grad certificate in ecosystem restoration and another in waste and environmental management."

Elias blinked at him. "Oh."

When nothing else was forthcoming, Ty gestured at Elias's empty plate. "You done with that?" Not waiting for a reply, he took it out of Elias's hands and walked it back up to the kitchen with his own.

God, he hated being made to feel small because of his job. He liked his job, liked knowing he was making a small difference in keeping the city he'd been born and raised in clean. Sure, replacing garbage bags in city trash cans and hauling full ones to the detainment centre wasn't what he wanted to do with the rest of his life. But it was a foot in the door that would eventually lead to one of the city's jobs in waste and environmental management. And getting his foot in the door had been *hard*—the city had a rigorous screening and interview process. He was damn lucky to be where he was.

Elias obviously hadn't meant to, but he'd hit one of Ty's hot buttons with his careless words. Just because he didn't work in a corner office in a downtown high-rise didn't mean his job wasn't beneficial and fulfilling. In fact, he could argue that, compared to Elias's, his job was *more* valuable. Keeping streets clear of trash and having comprehensive waste management systems in place to ensure proper waste prevention, recycling, and reusing was arguably more critical than assessing the needs of a company going through a reorganization.

One of the plates slipped out of his hands as he was depositing it in the sink to wash, splintering into thirds. It did nothing to help the irritation already pushing at the back of his throat, and he huffed in annoyance. Grabbing the largest piece, it again slipped out of his hands and back into the sink, leaving a two-inch gash on his palm.

Fuck. Seriously? Now he had a physical wound to add to his emotional one, and he so wasn't in the mood.

"Here."

Elias appeared next to him, turning on the cold water and maneuvering Ty's bleeding hand underneath the stream. Ty didn't need to be looked after. He could take care of himself. He didn't need Elias interfering in something he already had under control and wrestled his hand out of grasp.

"Stop," Elias said, voice firm.

Stilling, Tay stood tense while Elias let the cold water rain down on his hand, teeth grinding craters into each other, purposely averting his gaze from the sight of Elias's brown hand holding his own lighter one. Elias only held Ty's hand under the water for thirty seconds or so, and though the cut had stopped bleeding, Elias wrapped a dish towel around his hand anyway.

And he didn't let go. No, he cupped Ty's hand between his warm ones and ducked down to catch Ty's eyes.

"I'm sorry," he said, squeezing Ty's hand gently. "Truly, I didn't mean to offend. My only excuse is that I'm ignorant of the skills and education required to do your job or to get hired by the city."

"So, what?" Ty said. "The successful businessman thought he'd slum it with an uneducated shlump who hauls garbage around all day?" He regretted the words as soon as he said them. They were mean and vindictive, and *his* only excuse was that he was hurt and he wanted to hurt back.

But instead of getting angry and pulling away like Ty expected, Elias only squeezed his hand again and said, "Did I say that?" cool as you please. Ty sort of envied yet also hated his ability to remain logical in the face of an argument.

His sigh was miserable. "No, I'm sorry."

"I'm sorry, too," Elias said. He dropped Ty's hand and held out his own. "Friends?" His eyes were teasing, a slight smile on his lips.

Ty wanted to be more than friends, but, "Friends," he said and shook Elias's hand with his unhurt one.

Elias framed Ty's face in his hands, his eyes a curious mixture of tentative, teasing, and serious.

"More than friends?" he asked.

Ty smiled and rested their foreheads together. "More than friends."

Chapter Six

"I'm sorry, but...are you *firing* me?"

The woman sitting across the desk from Elias was the third person he was letting go today. She was in her mid-forties with curly brown hair pulled back in a ponytail. Her brown eyes glared at him so hard he half expected laser beams to incinerate him at any moment.

Elias had done enough firing in the past few years that he could tell the cryers from the take-it-lying-down types from the can-I-stay-on-in-a-different-capacity types. This woman was none of those. Despite her musical name, Melody Harwich was a fighter.

"Why isn't Johnson doing the firing?"

Elias schooled his face into impassivity, so the regret he was feeling wouldn't show all over it, and held up a folder. "I'm sorry," he said. "I'm not at liberty to discuss that. I can, however, discuss the severance package Sander's has put together for you—"

"*Severance* package? Who the hell do you think you are?"

"I'm—"

"I mean, I *know* who you are," she corrected herself.

The entire staff at Sander's Printing knew who he was. The management had insisted on introducing Elias and his staff when they'd first been brought on two months ago. *Let me introduce the team that's going to recommend which of you stays and which of you goes.*

That was always fun.

"Did *you* recommend he fire me?"

Elias had, in fact, recommended the opposite.

"No, ma'am, I—"

"I have been with Sander's for *twenty years.* Twenty. Years. Sander's and I had an unwritten agreement that I would do whatever the company asked of me, and in return, I would have a job for life." The tears came then but she blinked them away and pointed a finger in his face. "Then some new fuckwad owner comes along and decides that a system that was working perfectly well and *successfully*, I might add, needs 'reorganizing'?" She made actual air quotes.

Said new fuckwad owner was Dick Johnson—and yes, Elias got a kick out of the name every time. Johnson was in the process of acquiring several printing companies across the country. He'd bought Sander's from a retiring Glen Sander almost three months ago, and despite the business's success—Melody was right about that—he wanted to let almost everyone he'd inherited go to be replaced by a new, younger demographic.

Elias had fought for Sander's' employees until Johnson had stopped taking his calls. Explaining to the man that keeping his current employees would ensure not only success but also loyalty and commitment went in one of Johnson's ears and out the other. Why had Johnson hired Top Line, Ltd if he wasn't going to listen to any of their recommendations?

Elias was still trying to figure out the answer to that question.

"You know what?" Melody stood and took the folder off his desk. "You can tell Dick Johnson to stuff it. And *you* can stuff it, too." She slammed Elias's office door behind her.

Elias tried not to take her words personally, but it wasn't easy. Having to let people go was the worst part of his job and always succeeded in making him feel like total shit. It wasn't technically part of his job, and Top Line never signed a contract that specifically stated they would coordinate and perform any letting go. But sometimes the top brass—in this case, Dick Johnson—negotiated with Elias's higher ups for exactly that, because they were "too busy."

Translation: *We want to stay on the remaining employees' good sides, so we need Top Line to do the firing for us.*

It was both pathetic and cowardly.

He sagged back in his chair and rubbed his temples with a shaking thumb and forefinger. Once he made VP, this part of his job would go to someone else. That day couldn't come soon enough. If only the board would make a decision on who was going to be awarded the position.

A knock on his door drew him out of his thoughts. Rachel entered without waiting for an invitation. She wore a cream sleeveless shirt tucked into a navy pencil skirt despite the day's return to a temperature of minus forty. Sitting in Melody Harwich's recently vacated seat, she crossed her legs at the ankles and arched an eyebrow.

"So?"

Elias swallowed an irritated sigh. "So?"

"Do we have to do this every day? What did your horoscope say?"

"Oh."

God, he'd been so distracted by thoughts of Ty on his walk to work this morning that he hadn't thought to grab a newspaper and check his daily horoscope for Rachel. What he *had* remembered? Ty's hot chocolate and apple turnover, which he'd bought before remembering that Ty had the week off.

They sat now on the end of his desk, an arm's length away. Elias could've consumed them himself, but they reminded him of Ty and he liked the constant reminder of their unexpected weekend together.

"Hel*lo*." Rachel waved a hand in front of his face.

"Sorry," he said. "Got a lot on my mind."

"Yeah. I passed Melody Harwich in the hallway. She was pissed," Rachel sing-songed.

"Can you blame her?" Elias asked, not appreciating how Rachel made light of the situation.

"Not one bit. You enjoyed firing her, didn't you?"

What the hell had he ever said or done to make her believe that? Was it his resting douchebag face at work?

Rachel didn't wait for him to reply to a question she thought she already knew the answer to. "Are you going to tell me about your horoscope?"

"No,. I didn't grab the paper this morning."

"You could've looked it up online."

He could've, had he thought of it. He shrugged at her, wishing she'd go away and let him stew in the misery that always hit after firing someone.

"Anyway," she carried on. "Steve headed back to Montreal this morning. You missed your chance there."

Steve was the cousin she'd wanted to set him up with. But considering he hadn't wanted a chance in the first place...

"You two would've been perfect together." She sighed dreamily, or...lustily? Rachel was one of those women who got turned on at the thought of two guys together. But the thought of her getting turned on by *him* and some other guy? It totally freaked him out.

"A Capricorn and a Taurus. Couldn't get any better."

"What about a...Capricorn and a Capricorn?" he asked before he could think better of it. It'd occurred to him on his walk here this morning that both he and Ty were Capricorns.

Rachel sat up straight in her chair. "Did you meet someone?"

"No," Elias said, managing to keep a straight face. "Just curious."

"Well...Capricorn and Capricorn...they're not the best match. Two Capricorns probably wouldn't satisfy each other sexually, both too practical and rational to let themselves go like that."

Given Elias's thoroughly enjoyable weekend with Ty, Rachel's point was debatable.

"Each Capricorn has his or her own set of values. Things they believe in wholeheartedly that are set in stone, and if the other Capricorn—hell, if *anybody*—doesn't live up to those expectations..." She left the rest of her sentence hanging.

"And Capricorns are ambitious and competitive, so there'd probably always be this silent competition going on between two of them, which means it'd be hard for one to trust the other. Plus," Rachel continued, "Capricorns are intellectuals. And since they're so determined to pretend they don't feel anything and they keep emotions bottled up in order to remain calm and in control— " She shot a pointed look his way. "—two Capricorn lovers most likely wouldn't readily open up to each other, not until one feels safe and secure enough around the other to let their feelings be known."

It sounded a lot like he and Ty were doomed. But Ty had been pissed at him yesterday for his insensitive words about his job, and he hadn't been afraid to show it. Had the situation been reversed, had Ty inadvertently insulted *him*, Elias would've sat there, incommunicative, quietly stewing in his repressed anger, getting more and more tense until he needed to escape. Which meant, again, that Rachel's point was debatable.

What exactly made him and Ty different versions of a Capricorn? Ty, like Elias, had all of the base Capricorn traits. He was ambitious—Ty had told Elias about his desire for one of the city's few waste and environmental positions. He was competitive, responsible, smart, determined. He was extremely organized and detail-oriented: For his move on

Saturday, not only had every piece of furniture been labelled with the room it was going into, but every room had a sticky note identifying where said piece of furniture should be placed. Every box had been similarly labelled in addition to the piece of paper taped to the outside that itemized what was *in* the box. (Seriously with all of that organization, it was kind of funny that he hadn't been able to find the lube and condoms yesterday morning.) Plus, Ty had a running list of the things Major General Mom had reorganized without his consent.

But unlike Elias, he didn't deny his feelings, didn't sit on them until they burned a hole in his gut and made him want to scream. Was that difference between them a result of their different upbringings? Ty had been born into a family who loved him, who'd no doubt made him feel safe and secure, so that he'd never been afraid, never had to deny who he was or how he felt.

Rachel eventually left after Elias told her he had a meeting. Sometimes it was the only way to get rid of her, although today it was true. But he rescheduled it, and then he rescheduled the next one and the last one after that.

Sending a quick note to his staff to let them know he'd be off-site for the rest of the day, he powered down his computer, packed up his messenger bag, bundled himself up in his many layers, snagged Ty's apple turnover and now-cold hot chocolate, took the back stairs out of the building, and snuck out without being seen. Never able to concentrate after firing someone anyway, it was better if he got the hell out of there and recharged in his own space.

He was home fifteen minutes later, and it hit him that he didn't want to be here either. He wanted Ty's cozy house, Ty's infectious smile, Ty's ability to make him laugh. But how soon after leaving a more-than-friend's house after a weekend together was too soon to send a text? For possibly the first time in his life, Elias desperately wanted to talk to another person, and he didn't want to be alone.

Too bad he didn't know the etiquette of dating. If he had more guts, he'd hop in his car and drive over to Ty's, surprise him with lunch or something. Instead he brewed coffee, changed into sweats and a hoodie, and transferred the pictures he took yesterday over to his laptop. He hadn't lied when he'd told Ty that he hadn't taken that many...he only had a dozen, and ten of those were of Ty. He'd been too embarrassed to let Ty see them when he'd asked. The other two were pretty decent shots of a northern cardinal and a tiny chickadee, so he touched those up using his photo editing software, added his digital signature, uploaded them to his website, and submitted them to his contact at *CanadaBirds* magazine.

Then he went back to the images of Ty: Ty putting on his snowshoes, Ty showing Elias how to put on his own, Ty smiling, Ty pointing at a funny tree on the Starkey Hill trail, Ty's nostril and eye from when he'd tried to take a selfie of them.

The best one, by far, was the last one Elias took, Ty with his head thrown back in laughter as he lay in the snow next to Elias. It was in profile, yet the devilishness in his half-closed eyes couldn't be mistaken, and his nose was scrunched from laughter. Elias wasn't a portrait photographer by any means, but once he adjusted the contrast and definition and added a black and white filter, he had a decent portrait on his hands.

One he would share with no one ever.

Instead he transferred it to his phone and set it as Ty's contact image.

His email pinged, then pinged again thirty seconds later, and then again a minute and a half after that. The first was a summary of digital and physical prints he'd sold via his website in the last week: sixty-seven, down from what he'd sold over the holidays, which was to be expected, but still a decent amount for early January when everyone was paying off their holiday bills. The second email was from *Canada-Birds* letting him know they'd be using his chickadee image in this November's issue—it was the fastest he'd ever received a response after submitting an image for consideration in a publication. The third email...

Dear Mr. Hood,

We'd once again like to invite you to interview for an open position with CanadaTravels *magazine: Director of Photography. We are seeking a full-time, experienced photographer, and based on the many images you've submitted to* CanadaTravels *over the last several years, you clearly have extensive photography knowledge. We'd be delighted to speak with you about the position, which works very closely with our Creative Director, Martha Lloyd. Please see the attached document for a description of the position, salary and...*

Elias didn't need to look at the attachment. He knew what it would say based on the previous two times they'd tried to recruit him for this position. Martha Lloyd was an old friend from university and had been trying to get him to apply for the director of photography position for the past three months. They'd met for coffee twice, spoken over the phone a handful of times. Each time Elias had declined the role, not because he didn't want it...he did. He hadn't used his creative skills on a large-scale project since he'd been the photographer for his university's newspaper in his third and fourth years. And if he took a second to think about it, he'd admit he missed it. But he was fine with his current job and wasn't sure he was ready for a change. Despite the crap aspect of firing people on an almost weekly basis, Elias loved the team he worked with at Top Line, respected the upper management, did good work that was valued, and made great money. The director of photography position would mean a cut to his salary. In the grand scheme of things, it wasn't that big of a deal to him. He'd always been frugal, he had quite a significant nest egg saved up, and his only expenses were bills, his car, his condo, and food. He'd have no trouble living off a reduced salary, but he had to admit that the money he made at Top Line was nice.

Plus, like he'd told Ty, a better photographer than he might come in one day and swoop his position away from him. There was no job security. Although Ty *was* right: The same could be said for any job. Take Melody Harwich as an example. Twenty years and then poof! Job gone because some new fuckwad owner deemed it necessary to have a younger staff.

But no, he was going to stay where he was at Top Line. No sense quitting a company he'd been with for seven years and a potential promotion to VP in order to chase a child-hood dream.

He was halfway through writing a brief no-thank-you message when, unbidden, he flashed back to his eight-year-old self and to his foster dad gifting him a toy camera for his birthday. Saving the draft, he flagged the email to respond to later and logged out of his account. Putting the laptop away, he shook himself off and headed for the kitchen, where he brewed yet another pot of coffee and made himself some pick-me-up pancakes that he drowned in maple syrup.

———

Hours later, Elias was still sitting on the couch, binge-watching *Legend of Korra*, though it wasn't as fun without Ty. He'd switched from coffee to water, and since it was dinnertime, from pancakes to baked salmon and veggies.

And he finally texted Ty.

Hi.

Pathetic.

How are you?

Equally as pathetic. He'd spent all weekend talking to Ty, and now he couldn't send him a simple text without sounding like a stuffy eighty-year-old? What he really wanted to say was, *I've been thinking of you all day. I miss you. Can I come spend the night again?*

Of course, he didn't say any such thing.

Ty's text came in only two minutes later. *Hey! How was your day?*

It was fine. How was yours? Elias sent. He didn't bother telling Ty he'd left work early because he'd needed to be alone after firing somebody he didn't think should be fired in the first place, only to sit on his couch all day, eating and watching *Korra* like a sad, lonely loser. He'd kept an eye on his work phone for any important emails that needed immediate attention, but other than that he got absolutely no work done.

It was completely unlike him.

He kept all of this from Ty because although Ty hadn't said anything, it was pretty clear he didn't approve of what Elias did for a living, and Elias wasn't in the habit of complaining in order to garner sympathy. God, he hated people who did that.

The next text that came in from Ty was a picture of a small, four-seater wooden table and chairs set in his retro kitchen against the wall between the door and the fridge. *Got myself a kitchen table today. Happy birthday to me!*

Ty was the only person Elias knew who texted in full sentences with punctuation. It was amazing.

Is it your birthday today? Elias asked. Ty was celebrating his birthday with his family on Saturday, but when was his actual birthday?

No. Wednesday.

Elias opened up his laptop and got online. It was probably too early in their more-than-friends relationship to be getting each other gifts, but Elias couldn't *not* acknowledge Ty's birthday. Whether or not he actually gave Ty the present he picked out was, as of right now, undetermined. He would have to work up the guts first, talk with Ty some more, feel him out. But at least he would have it, just in case.

Got any plans for your birthday? Besides Saturday's party, I mean? Elias sent, mind half on the conversation and half on his negotiations with a seller on Etsy for express shipping that would get Ty's present here by Wednesday.

Nope. My best friend was supposed to come over, and we were going to go to lunch. But his daughter has the flu, so he'll probably have to cancel.

Should he offer to take Ty out for dinner on Wednesday? Was it too early to take someone who was more-than-friends out for their birthday? The only person he could think of to ask was his own best friend, but Kevin lived in Ireland and it was early morning there already. He wouldn't appreciate a 1:00 am text.

He was saved having to think any further about it when Ty texted again. *Wanna watch* Korra *with me?*

Um...

Elias didn't finish the sentence, since it was fairly obvious that it'd be hard to watch something together given they were in different locations.

Through FaceTime, silly :) said Ty. *You watch on your end, I'll watch on my mine.*

The phone rang. Ty's name and picture popped up on the screen. Elias smiled, finished paying for his purchase, and settled in to watch TV with Ty.

Chapter Seven

FOR THE FIRST TIME IN HIS LIFE, TY WAS AT A LOSS AS TO what to do with himself. All because he was distracted with thoughts of Elias and he couldn't concentrate on anything.

Doug, Ty's best friend since fifth grade, took him out for a birthday lunch this afternoon. His daughter was doing much better, but she was still weak from the flu, and Doug hadn't wanted to leave her long. He'd taken Ty to an all-day breakfast place—because breakfast food was the bomb—and then headed back to Toronto.

Ty's whole family had called him at various times throughout the day—his sisters, his brothers, his parents, his grand-parents, even a couple of cousins he was close to—to wish him a happy birthday. As soon as he'd been company-less with no further phone calls expected, he'd snuggled into the window seat in his bedroom with a book and settled down to read, which was exactly how he wanted to spend his birthday.

But he couldn't concentrate. Because Elias. Ty was replaying old conversations in his head for no other reason than to hear the man's voice in his mind. They'd spoken this morning—Elias had called between meetings. Ty wanted to text him, but he didn't want to bug him again so soon. What if Elias thought he was too clingy and needy to be worth it? Better to wait.

He wanted to invite Elias over so they could celebrate his birthday in typical new-relationship-honeymoon-phase style: under the sheets. But he would never do it. Had they been further into their relationship, Ty wouldn't't've hesitated. As it was, he was back to appearing clingy and needy, so he didn't invite Elias anywhere.

Even more than wanting him here tonight, though, Ty desperately wanted Elias to come to his birthday party at his parents' on Saturday. Elias never spoke about friends or colleagues or family. Granted, Ty had never asked, but the topic of family usually came up when two people started dating, often without any prompting from the other. It gave Ty the impression that Elias was all alone in the world, and it hurt Ty to think of Elias that way, with no one to rely on or confide in or call his own. Everybody needed a support network. Ty wanted to plunk Elias down in the middle of his family and have them love on him. The man needed that type of friendship in the worst way.

To invite Elias to his party, or not to invite him? That was the question. On the one hand, if Ty invited him and Elias didn't feel comfortable going, or if he simply didn't want to, it might push Elias away. On the other hand, if Ty *didn't* invite him but Elias was hoping for an invitation, it might make Elias think Ty wasn't as invested in their relationship as Elias was. Or might be. Whatever. It wasn't exactly like they'd talked about their relationship status beyond "more than friends."

Annoyed with his circling thoughts, he set his book aside and called Jenn, the most level-headed of his siblings.

"Who are we talking about?"

"Elias," Ty reiterated. "You met him on Saturday, remember?"

"Ah, yes, the aloof hottie."

Not inaccurate, but Ty still bristled at the description.

"You're dating that guy?"

The way she said it made it sound like Elias had two heads and feathers for hair. His chest burned with the desire to defend his man. "Why do you say it like that?" he asked.

Jenn paused, and Ty could practically see her trying to find the right words, fingers running through her short bob.

"He's not exactly your usual type," she said. "You tend to date people who are...friendlier."

Elias was plenty friendly once you got to know him.

"If you say so," Jenn commented when Ty said as much. "I trust your judgement. If you think he's worth it, I'm not going to bug you about it."

That right there was one of the reasons he'd called her and not his brothers or Maddie, who was a bit too young to provide the kind of advice he needed.

"As for Saturday," Jenn continued, "I don't know, Ty. Maybe... What if you asked him if you can ask him?"

Ty's eyes crossed trying to figure that one out, but he thought he got it.

"So, like, 'Hey, Eli, would it be all right if I invited you to my party on Saturday?'" he guessed.

"Yeah," said Jenn. "That way you're not inviting per se. You're asking if it's okay if you invite him. Less pressure, you know?"

That was...amazingly simple. Communication. Who would've thought?

"And also explain that you won't be mad, if he says no. Your relationship is still new, after all." She paused. "You wouldn't be mad, right?"

"No, of course not." Mad, no. Disappointed, yes. But he'd get over it, and he'd understand. He thought he was getting better at making heads and tails out of Elias's personality. From what he could tell, Elias wasn't a people person, and he didn't like big crowds. The crowd on Saturday would be huge and unfamiliar to him. Which was probably super scary to an introvert.

Hanging up with Jenn, he opened up his messaging app. *Hey Eli. I'd like to invite you to my birthday party this Saturday at my parents', but I'm not sure if I should given the newness of our relationship*—he erased the last five words—*we've just started dating*. Were they dating? He erased that last word. *Hanging out*. Too informal? Fuck. He erased it all and started over. *Hey Eli, would you like to come to my birthday party this Saturday? You can* say *no. I won't be mad*. Now it sounded like Ty *wanted* him to say no. Double fuck.

He needed to get the wording right, and he needed to do it now. It was Wednesday and his party was on Saturday, which meant if he invited Elias any later in the week, it would be last-minute and appear as if Ty had forgotten to invite him. That was no good.

Gah! Whoever said dating was fun was a big, fat, fucking liar.

Maybe an invitation to a sort-of last minute party couldn't be done via text. No, it *definitely* couldn't be done via text. Ty wouldn't be able to get his thoughts across properly, and he wouldn't be able to gauge Elias's reactions. What if he scared Elias away just by asking and never heard from him again?

When Elias had left on Sunday night, they'd made no plans to see each other again. And that was stupid, stupid, stupid. It meant the earliest they'd see each other was Monday morning when Elias passed him on his way to work. Unless Ty brought up getting together on Friday, and when he had Elias in front of him, *then* he could ask him about Saturday. But then he was back to leaving it to the last minute.

Banging his forehead against the window in frustration, breath fogging on the cool glass, he almost missed the knock at the front door. His window seat faced the front of the house, but it was directly over the front porch, blocking his view of the driveway. If someone had parked in it, he couldn't tell.

Maybe it was one of the neighbours come to welcome him to the neighbourhood. He already had a plate of homemade chocolate chip cookies from the couple who owned the soy farm across the street and homemade oatmeal raison muffins from the lady who owned the horse farm a kilometre south. God, please don't let it be his family coming to surprise him on his birthday.

It was neither a neighbour nor family. Ty knew his smile was mushy, likely resembling that of a lovesick puppy's, but Elias's matched his—though it was combined with a heavy dose of tentativeness—so he didn't feel too silly about it.

Reaching out, he cupped Elias's bearded face in his hands and brought his mouth down for a kiss. It was the softest kiss Ty'd ever given anyone. His heart beat so hard in his chest, and little wings of happiness and nervousness brushed his stomach. He couldn't help himself. He was just so happy to see him.

Mouths clinging, tongues dancing, Elias palmed Ty's back and pulled him in to his body. Elias's hands were gentle even as they held him firmly. The dichotomy of the warm air from the house at his back and the chill clinging to Elias's winter coat made Ty shiver. Elias was here, here, here! And Ty hadn't even had to do anything! Pulling back only an inch when he needed to breathe, Ty stayed plastered against Elias and met his liquid brown eyes.

"Hi," he whispered past the stupid nerves in his belly.

"Hi," Elias said, matching his whisper.

"What are you doing here?" Ty asked it with a smile, so Elias would know that it was totally, completely, one hundred percent okay that he'd shown up unannounced. Because Elias was exactly the person he'd wanted to see today.

"Um..." Elias looked adorably confused. "I'm not really sure. Just wanted to see you on your birthday."

It was the most honest and vulnerable thing Elias had said since they'd started this relationship/dating/hanging out/whatever this more-than-friends thing was, and Ty melted. Right there. At Elias's feet. A puddle of heart-shaped goo.

Ty stepped backward over the threshold and into the house, bringing Elias with him with a hand in his coat. Elias's mouth landed on his again as he used a foot to shove the door closed behind him. Without removing his mouth from Elias's, Ty unbuttoned his navy wool coat and pulled his dress shirt out of his pants so he could slip his hands underneath. The combination of hot skin and cold shirt made him moan. He licked into Elias's mouth, tasting a hint of coffee and a lot of Elias.

They stood next to the door, kissing without urgency like they had on Saturday when Elias had stayed over. But unlike on the weekend, Ty knew exactly where the lube and condoms were.

Kisses slowing, they separated only to smile stupidly at each other. That dazedly smitten look from Elias shot a bolt of fire into Ty's heart, and he stepped back toward the stairs, bringing Elias with him.

In Ty's bedroom they stripped each other, but since neither of them seemed to want to stop kissing, it was slow going, their hands getting tangled. It made them both laugh.

Naked, finally naked, Elias's beautiful, toned body on full display, Ty couldn't stop running his hands down his smooth skin. God, he wanted this so bad. Wanted Elias's skin on his, body on his, mouth on his. He craved him, wanted to inhale him. On his back on the bed, Elias on top of him, Ty wrapped his legs around Elias's waist. Not that Elias appeared to be going anywhere, but still.

Head tilting back as Elias kissed a path down his neck and across his collarbone, he got as far as Ty's nipple before Ty needed that mouth back on his. Palming the back of Elias's head, he brought him back up. Their gazes locked for a half second before their lips met and the heat in Elias's eyes...

Fuck. It sent a current of lava straight from Ty's belly down into his aching dick, which was trapped between their stomachs and desperate for attention.

When Elias let his lips go, his eyes traced over Ty's face, looking for all the world like he was trying to memorize him. The tenderness with which Elias was looking at him caused a lump to form in Ty's throat, and he let out a shaky sigh. He ran a hand through Elias's hair, marvelling at how, despite the use of gel to spike it up, it was still soft to the touch, not hard and sticky.

What *was* sticky? Ty's belly, which he could feel was streaked with a mixture of both their pre-come. As if by mutual agreement, they shot each other wicked grins and reached for the lube and condoms in the night stand. Elias had more maneuverability, so he got to them first.

As Elias slicked up a couple of fingers, Ty let his legs fall to the side and mentally told Elias to hurry. He almost came off the bed when those lubed fingers stretched his hole, and Elias bit down on his nipple at the same time.

"Mmmmph," Ty said through a moan. How had Elias figured out his little pain kink so goddamn fast?

He lost his breath when Elias pegged his gland, his whole body going rigid, pleasure stealing his thoughts. His nails dug into Elias's back.

"God, Eli, please."

Surprisingly, Elias listened. He was sheathed and lubed within seconds, thrusting into Ty in one smooth motion that had Ty biting his lip.

Stretching himself out over Ty, Elias tugged Ty's lip out from beneath his teeth and sucked it into his own mouth. Ty moaned and wrapped his legs around Elias's hips again. Elias threaded their fingers together next to Ty's head.

Then he moved, slowly at first, eyes never leaving Ty's. Ty felt that hooded, lust-filled look arrow right into his chest. It made him feel safe and wanted, and he tried to convey those feelings to Elias. Must've worked, because Elias's entire face softened and he brought his lips down to Ty's again.

It felt like he was surrounded by Elias in every direction, and he came undone at the thought, toes curling, shooting without ever having laid a hand on his dick. Elias was right behind him, tearing his mouth away to bury his face in Ty's neck.

Elias slumped on top of him, the best kind of weight on his chest, both of them breathing hard. Lifting his head, Elias looked at Ty, smiled, and said, "Happy birthday."

Chuckling, Ty hugged him close and kissed his cheek. Withdrawing gently, Elias got up and headed to the bathroom. He came back with a warm washcloth and wiped Ty down, then threw the cloth into a corner and snuggled up to Ty.

"Don't fall asleep on me," he said when Ty laid his head on his shoulder.

"I won't," Ty reassured. His eyes fell closed.

"I'm serious," Elias said, giving him a nudge. "Don't you want your birthday present?"

Ty opened one eye, curious. "Are you just saying that to keep me awake?"

"Don't you want to find out?"

Yes, damn it.

Elias hopped out of bed, yanked on his suit pants and coat and disappeared downstairs.

"Don't fall asleep while I'm gone!" he yelled before the front door open and slammed close.

Ty snorted and made no promises.

Elias was back within a minute, shivering, holding a cloth grocery store bag. Stripping quickly, he settled himself against the headboard, pulling the covers up to his waist. Ty sat up next to him, otherwise he really would fall asleep.

Elias pulled a small gift bag out of the cloth one and handed it over.

"Happy birthday."

"You really did get me a gift." Ty couldn't help his delighted smile. He'd expected a text from Elias this morning. Instead he'd gotten a mid-morning phone call, a surprise house visit, birthday sex, *and* a gift? Who was this Elias, and how did Ty ensure he didn't disappear?

Yanking out the tissue paper, he reached in for the present and—

"I love it!"

It was a white mug with a picture of a young Korra and the phrase "I'm the avatar. You gotta deal with it!" which were the first words Korra said in *Legend of Korra*.

He couldn't help but laugh. "Seriously, this is great. Where'd you find it?"

"Etsy," Elias said. "But that's, um..." For some reason he looked nervous. "It's more like a gag gift."

"Gag gift? Are you kidding? This is my new hot chocolate mug."

Elias smiled, but it lacked its usual killer punch. He reached once again into the cloth bag and pulled out a flat, square package, roughly eight by ten. Colour high on his cheekbones, Elias hesitated another second before handing it over. Ty set the mug on the nightstand so he could take it.

"This is your actual gift," Elias said.

His nerves made Ty all the more curious, but he was careful tearing the wrapping from his present, conscious that this—whatever it was—was important to Elias.

Ty gasped when he got a look at the black-and-white image in the heavy, wooden frame. It was him. In profile, taking up about two-thirds of the photograph, head thrown back in laughter, laugh lines around his eyes, nose scrunched.

"This... When..." Overwhelmed, he couldn't even find

words. This picture was obviously one Elias had taken. And he was sharing it with Ty.

"On Sunday," Elias said.

When they'd gone snowshoeing.

"I..."

Joy. That was what this picture conveyed—joy and freedom and love and a wild sense of belonging and security.

"It's how I see you," Elias quietly admitted.

Tears came, fast and unexpected, because although Elias didn't talk about himself much, didn't share his feelings, his hopes and dreams... This gift, it was everything Elias couldn't say, wrapped up for Ty to either accept or reject. The courage it must've taken for him to share something so personal...

Ty set the frame on the pillow next to him and crawled into Elias's lap to hug the shit out of him.

"Hey," Elias said, hands soothing up and down Ty's back. "Why are you crying?"

"Fuck you, I'm not," Ty said, voice choked.

"Oh." Elias smiled against his neck. "My apologies."

Ty pressed a series of kisses to Elias's face, making him chuckle softly, and then cupped his hands around his jaw, rubbing his thumbs on Elias's stubbled cheeks.

"Thank you." *For the gift, for showing yourself to me, for giving yourself to me.*

"You're welcome," Elias said.

And Ty swore some of those walls came down.

TWENTY MINUTES LATER, TY WAS DRINKING HOT chocolate out of his new birthday mug while Elias called a Thai restaurant in Guelph for delivery. They were both starving, and neither wanted to cook. It was dinnertime and—

Doing a double-take, Ty's eyes practically bugged out of

his head at the time on the microwave. 5:30 pm? He checked the time on the stove to confirm. Well, shit. Elias had already been here for an hour and a half at least, which meant he must've left work early, three o'clock, if not earlier to beat the traffic.

There Ty went, getting all gooey and lovesick again. His high-powered guy, who was angling for the open VP position at his company, had cut out of work early to come see him.

"What are you smiling at?" Elias asked, putting his phone down on the table. He looked seriously hot in a pair of suit pants and nothing else.

"Nothing," Ty said, nabbing a cookie from the plate between them. "Just thinking that you're hot."

Elias grunted, like, *yeah, I know.*

"You're going to spoil your appetite with those," he said.

"Doubtful," Ty said, polishing off his cookie in two bites. "It's just sugar, and that's not filling. Besides, it'll be, what, an hour before they deliver?"

"Yup, or we can pick it up in half an hour."

"That'd be much more tempting if it wasn't minus a billion outside."

"It's minus seven at the most," Elias corrected.

"Minus a billion with the windchill," Ty said, standing firm.

Elias just laughed at him.

"Do you want a beer?" Ty asked him.

"No, I'm good, thanks," Elias said, stealing a sip from Ty's mug.

Ty gasped in mock outrage. "Thief!"

Elias moaned at the taste of the hot chocolate, the sound shooting into Ty's balls. "Damn, this is good."

"'Cause I use real chocolate pieces instead of powder."

"Huh." Elias took another sip. Ty glared at him. "How was

your day?" Elias asked, not giving Ty his mug back. "Did your friend come for lunch?"

"Yeah, we went to an all-day breakfast place in Guelph."

Those damn brown eyes of Elias's twinkled with humor as he continued to sip *Ty's* hot chocolate out of *his* cool new mug.

"Gonna make me a new one?" Ty asked, nodding at the mug in Elias's hands.

"Nope." Elias shot him a sunny smile. "You're the expert."

Pretending to grumble under his breath, Ty got up to make himself a new drink.

"I wanna use my new mug." Ty stuck out his bottom lip in a pout.

"Tough," Elias said. "And anyway, technically it's mine since I bought it."

Ty pointed a wooden spoon at him. "I hate your logical mind."

Elias laughed. "Says the guy who had post-its everywhere on moving day?"

"Hey, that's just simple organization, and I made everyone's lives easier."

Except his own. All because his mother insisted on reorganizing based on her own sense of how a home should look. But he'd kept a running list of everything she'd moved and had spent the last two days putting things to rights. Which meant he now had the next four days free to do nothing but sit in his window seat and read and drink hot chocolate.

Well, three days free. He had his own birthday party on Saturday, which reminded him...

"Eli..."

"Yeah?" came Elias's voice in his ear, making Ty jump. Elias's arms came around his waist, and a kiss landed on his shoulder. "What's up?" Elias asked, voice rumbly and warm in Ty's ear.

"Erm..." Ty focused on stirring the milk warming in the saucepan.

Elias leaned sideways and peer at him.

"Why are you looking at me like that?" Ty asked.

"Since when are you ever at a loss for words?"

Elias had a point, but Ty hadn't had a chance to rehearse or to come up with the perfect wording.

"I just...uh..." He added the chocolate pieces to the milk and continued to stir. "You know my parents are throwing me a birthday party on Saturday?"

"Uh-huh."

"Do you maybe want to come? You don't have to...if you don't want... I get that we just started...uh...this, so I won't be mad or anything, if you don't want to."

Now Elias looked even more confused. "I don't understand," he said. "Do you want me to come, or do you not want me to come?"

Yeah, Ty could see how what he'd said would make no sense to anybody but him. His throat closed off, a sure sign he was getting annoyed with himself. Removing the saucepan from the stovetop, he turned in Elias's arms to face him.

Running his hands up and down Elias's biceps, he went with honesty and hoped it didn't kick him in the ass.

"The truth is, I would love for you to come. But I know we just started this...thing...dating...whatever this is, and I don't know if it's too soon to invite you to a family function."

"I don't know if it's too soon either," Elias said, thumbs hooking into the top of Ty's boxers. "To be honest, I don't have a lot of relationship experience. The last time I had an actual boyfriend was in my first and second years at Queen's, and that was quite a while ago."

Did that mean he thought of Ty as a boyfriend? Damn those stupid butterflies in his tummy making him feel like a twittering teen. He squeezed Elias's arms, sincerely hoping he was right.

"Since then," Elias continued, "it's been casual hookups, nothing important, not like this." His smile was a bit rueful. "I've also been worrying about doing the right thing, wondering if I'm going too fast, but... What if we just stop? Stop pretending we know what we're doing or not doing, stop worrying about rushing or not rushing and just...go at our own pace, whatever that might be for us?"

What was with all the honesty Elias was throwing at him today? It was making Ty's heart do funny things in his chest.

"That sounds perfect," Ty said. "Because I have no idea what I'm doing." They just had to be honest with each other. Hopefully it would help cut back on the anxiety they both seemed to be feeling.

"That surprises me," Elias said.

"What does?"

"That you don't know what you're doing," Elias explained. "I don't understand why guys haven't been lining up at your door, waiting to take you out."

Ty snorted. He'd always been picky, so sue him. "I could say the same about you," he pointed out.

Elias grunted. "I would love to come to your party," he said, changing the subject.

"Yeah?" Ty smiled wide. "You don't have to, you know."

"Are you trying to convince me not to?" By the look in his eyes and the smile he couldn't hide, Elias obviously meant it as a joke.

"No, I just don't want you to be uncomfortable."

"First time meeting a whole bunch of new people?" Elias said, one eyebrow raised, like, *and you expect me* not *to be uncomfortable?* It was amazing how loudly his non-verbal body language spoke. "How many people will be there?"

Ty hesitated, trying to think of a number that wouldn't

overwhelm Elias. But he had a feeling that number was five or less, and since there were going to be way more than five people at his parents' house on Saturday, he opted for honesty again and hoped for the best. "Twenty-five?"

Elias's eyes went wide. "How do you know so many people?"

"It'll be mostly family," Ty reassured. Brothers, sisters, in-laws, parents, nieces and nephews, grand-parents, cousins, aunts and uncles. Throw in a few friends popping in randomly throughout the day. To someone like Elias, who didn't seem to have any family, it probably did sound like a lot.

"Hey, when's your birthday?" Ty asked Elias.

"On the first," Elias said. He pecked Ty's lips quickly and returned to the table.

"A New Year's baby?" Ty turned back to the stove to finish making his hot chocolate. "That must be lucky."

Elias laughed, a harsh, grating sound that lacked anything resembling amusement, a blunt-edged knife that clawed at Ty's insides. "Not really."

Ty turned. Elias stared hard into his mug, rubbing his jaw with one hand.

"Eli?"

Brown eyes flicked up to Ty's then away. The hand on his mug spasmed briefly before he got it under control.

"My mom left when I was two," he said. "When I was five, my dad went to jail for selling drugs to minors. He died in there three months later."

Turning off the burner, Ty abandoned his hot chocolate and sat at the table across from Elias.

"My sister and I were put into foster care since we didn't have any other family," Elias continued. "But because Amira's six years older than me, they split us up and sent us to different homes, to ones with kids our own age."

Ty swallowed hard and reached for Elias's hand. "I'm sorry," he said.

"Don't be." Elias rubbed his thumb over the back of Ty's hand. "It was a long time ago."

"Was foster care..."

Elias smiled at that. "It wasn't as bad as the stories you hear. I bounced around from family to family for the first couple years, no placement lasting longer than a few months. Then just before my eighth birthday, I got placed with the Hoods. They adopted me two years later."

Oh, thank God there was some good to this story.

"What are they like?" Ty asked.

"They were great," Elias said, smile fond as he played with Ty's fingers. "First thing they did when the adoption went through was take me to Disney World. It's still my favourite place in the world."

They *were* great, Elias said. Did that mean...

"Do you still talk to them a lot?" he asked, tentative, not wanting to summon bad memories yet desperately needing to know.

"No," Elias said, voice whisper-soft. "That plane crash three years ago, between London and Paris?"

Ty put two and two together, his shoulders slumping.

Elias's smile was sad as he correctly read Ty's reaction. "They were on it."

"God! Can't you catch a break?" Ty's voice was garbled with tears, and he swiped at his burning eyes. "Life sucks sometimes."

"Yeah," Elias agreed. "But I turned out all right, didn't I?"

It was ridiculous that Elias was trying to comfort Ty when it should be the other way around. Ty sucked up his tears and walked around the table to straddle Elias's lap. Putting his arms around Elias's shoulders, he buried his face in his neck and held on tight.

"Don't be sad, baby," Elias said. His voice was strong, but he held Ty just as tightly. "I'm okay."

Ty could argue that point, but he didn't. He sniffled and pulled back.

"Are you close with your sister, at least?" he asked.

"No," Elias answered, hands smoothing up and down Ty's thighs. "We weren't close even as kids. She moved to Vancouver for university when she was eighteen and never came back. We talk on the phone every once in a while, but it's always like talking to a stranger."

Ty patted Elias's hard shoulders. "You can have some of my family," he offered. "They'd take you."

"I don't know if I want your family," Elias said. "They're kind of crazy."

Ty's laugh was half snort, half sob. "Wait until you meet the rest of them on Saturday."

The horror that widened Elias's eyes was hilarious. Ty laughed even though a part of him still hurt so much for Elias and everything he'd gone through. Leaning forward, he captured Elias's lips with his, kissing him slowly, hoping to convey to him that he was safe here with Ty. Pulling back, he frowned into Elias's eyes.

"You taste like my hot chocolate," he grumbled.

Elias chuckled and leaned in for another kiss. "Want some more?"

"No," Ty said, laughing, pushing Elias away. "I want my own."

"No, you want mine."

Yeah, he did.

Chapter Eight

"DO YOU WANNA COLOUR WITH ME?"

God, did he ever.

Elias followed the pig-tailed five-year-old over to the kids' play area in the den, where most of the children had congregated to play. A couple of pre-teens were playing a video game—something with lots of bloopy noises—and three pint-sized girls were playing house over by the plastic kitchen playset.

The five-year-old handed him a Harry Potter colouring book, pointed at a box of coloured pencils, and sat in a child-sized chair at the child-sized table. Elias sat on the floor across from her, which put the table at mid-chest. Perfect colouring height for him.

Too bad he hadn't found the den an hour ago, when the press of so many bodies in the Green house started to be too much. He could handle introducing himself and talking about himself for only so long before he lost the will to live. Luckily, midway through the arrivals, he'd discovered a trick. If he began the conversation with "So, what do you do?" instead of the other way around, then all he had to do was pick apart their answer and jump on a second topic. "Oh, you're an electrician? How did you get in to that?" It was brilliant, because by the time the other person's explanation ran down, Elias was being introduced to someone new who'd just arrived, and he could start the cycle all over the again. It meant, in essence, that he barely had to say anything at all.

Ty was in his element as he accepted birthday wishes from his family and friends. Every guest who arrived gave him a huge hug and pressed a gift into his hands. Yet there was a certain tightness to Ty's eyes that told Elias what he really wanted was to crawl into a corner and read.

Elias could relate.

"Ah," Ty said from the doorway. "There you are." He sat next to Elias, bracing himself with one hand on Elias's shoulder. "Hannah, can I draw, too?" he asked the pig-tailed girl. She handed over a *My Little Pony* colouring book.

Ty took one look at it then leaned over to see what Elias was drawing. His eyes lit up. "Trade you?"

Elias looked at his half-coloured Hogwarts crest. "No." He moved his book out of Ty's reach.

Ty pouted. It shouldn't have been adorable on a grown man; somehow Ty pulled it off. However, it seemed that Ty didn't actually want to colour. He tested out four shades of pink for his pony. Unhappy with them, he switched to purple. Then he flipped through the pages of his book for a different page to colour. Apparently unsatisfied, he set it aside and grabbed a different one: *Despicable Me*. Apparently, he didn't like that one either.

"What's wrong with you?" Elias asked, straight to the point. Ty was not normally a fidgeter.

"Do you want to see my room?" Ty said instead of answering.

Why yes, yes he did.

"Bye, Hannah," he said. It was only appropriate since she'd invited him to colour with him in the first place. She ignored him.

They had to pass by the packed living room on their way; luckily no one stopped them. Jenn was the only one who caught them, but she simply waved and went back to her conversation.

"You're in the basement?" Elias asked as Ty took them downstairs.

"Yeah. I moved down here when my parents finished it when I was in high school."

Ty's bedroom walls were blue, his carpet a thick cream. It was also empty. Made sense seeing as he'd just moved all of his things to his new house. There was nothing to see, so why had Ty bought him down here?

Ty stretched out on the couch outside his bedroom, and Elias joined him, snuggling Ty close so he didn't fall off the edge. Ty's restless fingers played the piano on Elias's chest in an irritating rhythm. Elias threaded their fingers together.

"Are you okay?" he asked again.

"Yeah," Ty said. "Just...too many people."

They lay together in the semi-darkness, the only light coming from the basement windows. Party sounds filtered through the ceiling: children screaming, a crying baby, a thud as something was dropped, and above it all, the din of a dozen conversations. They didn't speak, didn't move. Simply lay quietly, enjoying each other's company, breathing each other in. Elias's other hand was around Ty's waist, and he snuck it under Ty's T-shirt, wanting to feel his warm skin. Ty shivered and pressed closer.

Elias released a long breath, his muscles unclenching. Alone with Ty, he could finally relax. Didn't have to be *on*. It surprised him that Ty felt the need to escape his own family and friends, but maybe like Elias, he preferred people in small groups and small doses.

"How long will the party last?" Elias asked.

"Oh, probably until eleven or so."

Oh, God.

"Don't worry." Ty patted his chest. "Jenn and my dad will sneak us out of here in about an hour."

God bless Ty's only normal family members.

A creak as the basement door opened. Ty moaned a protest.

"I don't think he's down here," a voice said. One of Ty's brothers.

"Jenn said she saw him head this way." That was the other twin.

"If you say so."

"Besides, where else would he hide?"

They appeared at the bottom of the stairs, dressed similarly in dark jeans and polo shirts. Ty had told him that they lived next door to each other and shared a big backyard. Elias couldn't tell which was which yet, but he knew Matt called everybody "dude." He felt like he should sit up—wouldn't it be weird for them if they saw he and Ty cuddled together? But Ty didn't move, so Elias stayed where he was.

"Dude."

Ah, so the one in the purple polo was Matt. Jeremy was the one in green.

"Aunt Liza thinks your new boyfriend's hot."

Ty chuckled and finally sat up. Elias did the same, propping himself up in the corner between the arm and the back of the couch.

"Which one was she?" Elias asked.

"The one with the cane," Ty said.

"The four-hundred-year-old?"

That cracked the brothers up and neither one of them refuted his claim. The four-hundred-year-old in question was a tiny, stooped lady with wrinkles on her wrinkles.

"She patted my cheek like I was a disobedient toddler earlier," Elias grumbled.

Ty laughed so hard he fell over on the couch, making Elias smile at him like a sentimental fool.

The door opened and closed again, soft footsteps descending the stairs.

"Maddie, did you bring cake?" Jeremy called.

Ty's teenage sister did indeed bring cake. The whole cake.

What was left of it anyway. And given it'd been huge to begin with, there was a little less than half left. She set the cake dish on the floor and handed out forks.

Jenn found them five minutes later, lying on their stomachs in a circle around the dish, picking at the triple chocolate fudge cake with three layers of icing.

"Where's my fork?" she asked.

Maddie held one out to her and she dug right in with the rest of them.

The doorknob jiggled at the top of the stairs.

"I locked it behind me," Jenn told Ty.

"I love you," he said, stuffing his face with a huge bite of cake.

"Mom's going to come looking for us eventually," Maddie said.

"She's currently occupied trying to get Kylie to clean the drawing she made on the wall in the kitchen," Jenn said.

Jeremy groaned. If Elias remembered correctly, Kylie was his toddler.

"I *told* Mom not to put the whiteboard against the wall," he said.

"Maybe she thought your daughter was smarter than you and could distinguish between a drawing surface and a non-drawing surface," Ty said.

"Why would any child of Jeremy's be smart?" Matt joked.

"Says the guy whose son tried to toast yogurt," Jenn quipped.

"I'm sorry, whose six-year-old tried to plug in a book?" Matt said to her.

"Children are the root of all misery," Jeremy said philosophically.

It was fun to watch them banter back and forth. Elias had never had this kind of relationship with his sister, and he'd been careful not to get too attached to any of the foster kids that came while he lived with the Hoods, knowing they could be removed and placed elsewhere with barely a moment's notice. In the back of his mind, he hadn't really believed that Ty's sitcom-type family actually existed; one where the parents were still alive and together and the siblings were friends as well as family.

They polished off the rest of the cake. It was impressive how much the Green siblings could eat. When there was only a small corner left, Elias forked it closer to Ty. It was his birthday cake after all. Ty bumped his shoulder with his in thanks. Jenn smiled at him, Maddie pretended not to notice, and the twins made big doe eyes and pretended to swoon.

"Just for that," Ty told his brothers, "you don't get my sushi gift card."

"Awww."

"No fair."

"Aunt Margo is *still* getting you a gift card to that sushi place?" Maddie asked. "How does she not know yet that you don't eat sushi?"

"But we got you such a great gift." Matt was still complaining.

"Yeah, isn't that worth a twenty-five-dollar sushi gift card?" Jeremy said.

"You haven't given me anything," Ty said through a laugh.

It gave the twins pause. They met eyes, had some kind of silent conversation, and by apparent mutual agreement, Jeremy disappeared upstairs.

"So, Maddie." Matt's devilish tone made them all pause. "Where's *your* boyfriend?"

Maddie narrowed her eyes at her brother.

"Boyfriend?" Jenn asked.

"What boyfriend?" Ty asked.

"There's no boyfriend," Maddie said, colour high in her cheeks.

"I caught them kissing in the shed last night," Matt sang.

"The shed? Ew," Ty said and shuddered hard.

"There are centipedes in there," Jenn said.

"We were not *kissing*," Maddie insisted.

"Really?" said Matt. "Then what would you call the art of thrusting one's tongue down another person's throat?"

"Tonsil hockey," Elias suggested.

"Making out," Ty said.

"Sucking face," Matt said.

"Canoodling," Jenn said.

A growl released from the back of Maddie's throat. "I hate you all."

"So? Where is he?" Ty asked.

"Yeah, how come you didn't invite him?" Jenn poked Maddie's shoulder with her fork.

"Because he's not my boyfriend," Maddie said. "He's just a friend, who's also a boy."

"A *kissing* friend who's a boy," Matt clarified.

"How come he's not your boyfriend?" Ty asked. "What's wrong with him?"

"There's nothing *wrong* with —"

"Then my question stands," Ty interrupted. "How come he's not your boyfriend?"

"Because he's...he's..." She seemed to be searching for an excuse. "He's not a good kisser."

Silence.

Then, "If he's not a good kisser," Jenn started, "you were doing what while he was kissing you? Counting his teeth with your tongue?"

"Can you do that?" Ty asked.

"We can try it out later," Elias promised.

Ty beamed at him.

"Awww," Jenn said, smiling indulgently at them. "You guys are cute."

Jeremy reappeared, envelope in hand. Ty's gift presumably. "What'd I miss?"

"Maddie has a boyfriend," Matt said.

Maddie's forehead hit the floor.

TURNED OUT, IT WAS RATHER DIFFICULT TO COUNT another person's teeth with one's tongue. It was hard to tell where one tooth ended and another began, but Ty gave it his best shot anyway.

After the party Ty had driven Elias back to his condo on Queen's Quay, fully expecting Elias to kiss him goodnight and then wave him off so Ty could drive home alone. But Elias had invited him inside. To spend the night. Ty had packed an overnight bag this morning, hoping for exactly this outcome. Presumptuous?

"No," Elias said when Ty told him. "Smart."

Ty was glad he thought so.

Two hours later, thoroughly fucked, feeling languid and loose, he was happy to spend some time exploring Elias's mouth. Lying side by side, legs tangled underneath the covers, Elias's tongue in his mouth tasting of chocolate and coffee, Ty felt sinful and wanted.

"I'm surprised you're not asleep yet," Elias murmured, hand in Ty's hair.

"I make no promises for what the next five minutes hold," Ty said. He was too sleepy and sated not to fall asleep, no matter how much he wanted to stay awake and talk to Elias all night.

"I think I can tempt you into wakefulness," Elias said.

"Yeah?" Ty's smile was naughty, and his dick gave a twitch.

"Not with that," Elias said, laughing. "Come with me."

They put on boxers before Elias led Ty to the second

bedroom he used as an office. Elias's condo faced the lake, almost directly across from the island airport, and Ty was momentarily distracted by the airport lights.

Until he realized why Elias had brought him in here.

"Eli..." His heart froze then started to pound. Framed pictures hung on the walls, landscapes and wildlife photos with Elias's digital signature in the bottom right. They were incredible: the northern lights, a herd of bison in the prairies, a lone wolf, fall in Algonquin Park, a pair of swans, a hummingbird, snow-capped Rockies, an owl in flight. All with an ethereal quality that made them look more like paintings than prints.

"These are amazing," he whispered. He reached to touch but yanked his hand back, afraid of leaving smudges on these works of art.

"This one's going to be in *CanadaTravels* in September." Elias pointed at the Algonquin Park image.

"That's...that's the number one travel magazine in the country," Ty said, amazed.

"Yeah," Elias said, like it was no big deal. "That one—" He pointed. "—was in a past issue. This one's on their website." He kept naming websites and magazines his images had appeared in, including some big name ones that had Ty's jaw dropping.

"Remind me again why you don't do this full time?" Ty asked.

Elias shrugged. "I've been with Top Line for seven years."

There was a non-answer if Ty'd ever heard one. How was that even a legitimate reason for not following a dream? Because it was clear that *this* was Elias's passion. His face lit up, eyes gleaming, as he spoke about the photographs, how he'd gotten certain shots, the patience associated with wildlife photography, how fun it was to tweak RAW images, the rush he still felt whenever a publication accepted one of his submissions or he sold a print off his website.

It was the first Ty was hearing of a website, and when his gaze landed on Elias's laptop, sitting innocently on the desk, Elias read his mind. With an indulgent roll of his eyes and a slight smile, he powered it up, navigated to his website, and turned the laptop toward Ty.

Ty went through his online gallery for who knew how long. At one point, Elias disappeared. He came back with a hoodie for Ty, who hadn't realized he'd been sitting there in boxers and goosebumps. Left again. Returned with hot chocolate.

"Are you hungry?" he asked.

"Go away," Ty said. "I'm busy."

Elias snorted a laugh and left.

Why, why, why was Elias not working as a full-time photographer for some website or magazine? Why didn't he take more freelance jobs? The job security excuse Elias had once given was a crock of shit. More like Elias had certain ideals that he lived by, and part of those ideals dictated how he should live, what sort of job he should have, how much money he should make, what kind of home he should live in. It wasn't Elias's fault. Likely it had something to do with how he was raised and everything he'd gone through before being adopted. His mother gone, his dad shipped off to prison, Elias shuffled from one home to another until he was adopted by loving parents, who were killed in a plane crash. In Elias's world, probably nothing felt permanent, everything easily breakable, easily taken away, like sand slipping through his fingers.

But the money he made? It was his. Nobody could take it away. His job? Elias had worked his way up to that position. Elias's condo, his car? All paid for with the money he made at a job Ty suspected Elias didn't even like but that he was used to and good at and where people respected him. If Elias quit his job and started a new one that went to shit, it might mean a loss to his savings. Goodbye, car. Goodbye, condo. Gone as if they'd never existed. And he was back to being that little boy—hell, the adult—who'd had everything taken away from him.

Ty's vision blurred. The lump in his throat choked off his air, and he sobbed once before getting it together. He didn't want Elias to hear, to know how much he hurt for him, how much he wished he could fix things. But the only one who could change the way Elias thought, what he believed, was Elias himself. All Ty could do was stick by him, show him that not everybody left.

Chapter Nine

Capricorn, romance is in the air. Venus—the planet of love—will be visible to the naked eye for the next two weeks—until Valentine's Day! If there's a special someone in your life, it's a good time to tell them how you feel.

TWO WEEKS LATER THE EARLY FEBRUARY TEMPERATURE showed no sign of warming up. If anything, it got colder, and Mother Nature dumped almost six feet of snow on the GTA in the span of three days.

Elias took a picture of his Saturday horoscope on his laptop screen and texted it to Rachel before he poured the milk into his bowl of flour.

"You never check your horoscope anymore," she'd said yesterday morning at the office. Instead of grabbing a newspaper on his way to work, he and Ty now spent thirty minutes chatting every morning at the café. They were such regulars over the past two weeks that the morning baristas knew their orders by heart.

Of course, he didn't tell Rachel any of that. Just told her he was sorry, and he'd do better, because it was easier than telling her about Ty and having to answer the five hundred questions about him she'd shoot his way.

Too bad you don't have a special someone in your life, she texted back, complete with a sad-face emoji. Was she being sarcastic? Had Elias somehow given himself away, and now she suspected he was seeing someone? Not likely. She would've included one of those winking emojis instead of a sad-face

one, all *I know your secret*. He could almost hear her singsongy
voice in his head.

Adding an egg, sugar, baking powder, and salt to his
batter, he stirred it smooth.

You'll be all alone on Valentine's Day, Rachel sent now. Oh,
how little she knew.

"I did it," Ty said, coming into the kitchen.

"Yeah?" Dressed in his typical after work/weekend/lazing
around the house outfit of boxers and a hoodie, Ty looked
like the eighteen-year-old Elias had first thought him to be
weeks ago. "Congratulations."

Ty scoffed and took a seat at the island. "Don't congratu-
late me yet. All I did was hit Submit on the online
application."

"Still. How do you feel?"

"Anxious."

Ty didn't meet his eyes, instead reaching for the bowl of
grapes.

"Why?"

A head shake.

"Ty."

Blue eyes lifted to his.

"What's going on?"

Ty's tight-lipped smile was both embarrassed and
confused. "This just wasn't part of the plan, you know? I was
going to work this job for a few years then work my way up to
a position in waste management with *this* city."

"Well, you don't really have to worry about anything yet,"
Elias pointed out. "Like you said, all you've done is apply.
There's no guarantee they'll hire you. Hell, there's no guarantee you'll get an interview." He purposely played devil's
advocate, wondering how Ty would feel if nothing came of
this. By the frown on Ty's face, he didn't like that thought so
much.

"Still," Ty said around the grape in his mouth. "I feel like the past two years working for the city will have been for nothing."

The city of Guelph was hiring for some kind of junior waste management role. Ty's supervisor at his current job knew one of the hiring managers and had recommended him for the position, which meant of course he'd get an interview. Referrals were everything in business. Ty just had to get it through his head that even though it wasn't a position with the city of Toronto, it was an office position in waste management nonetheless, one where he'd be putting his certificate in waste management to practical use instead of simply emptying garbage cans downtown. As a bonus, the commute to Guelph would only be fifteen minutes instead of the almost hour and a half it currently took him to get to work.

"That's not true," Elias countered. He set his batter aside and sat across from Ty. "Every job teaches a new skill, whether it's hard skills like how to change a flat tire or soft skills like time management."

Ty wasn't convinced.

"Or maybe things were meant to happen this way," Elias continued. "Maybe you were meant to work for the city, so that the role could put you in front of this particular supervisor who would then recommend you for a position you're extremely qualified for in the field you love."

Ty was looking at him like he had goop on his face. "*Meant* to...?" he said, brow furrowed. "That's not very logical of you."

Elias laughed and got up to retrieve a pan from the cupboard. "True. Must be all the wishy-washy horoscopes I've been reading lately."

"What did it say today?" Ty asked. Elias had told him about his morning conversations with Rachel over a week ago.

"Something about Valentine's Day." He didn't mention

the whole tell-your-someone-special-how-you-feel-about-them part. Just thinking about telling Ty how he felt about him made him break out in a cold sweat.

"Ugh," Ty said. "Valentine's Day is stupid."

"Oh, thank God," Elias said with a groan. "I was worried we were going to have to go all out for it." He set the pan on the burner to warm.

"The most I want from you on Valentine's Day is a blow job," Ty said, eyebrows wagging. "And a bottle of chocolate sauce, so I can lick it off you."

Elias's dick twitched at the thought, nipples hardening. He pointed his spatula at Ty. "Sold! To the gentleman in blue boxers!"

Ty took a bow like he'd won the grand prize. "What are you making anyway?"

"Pancakes."

Ty's eyes went comically wide. "From scratch?"

"How else do you eat pancakes? Do *not* say frozen," Elias added when Ty opened his mouth to respond. He wisely stayed silent, mouth pressed in a tight line so he wouldn't laugh.

"What are we doing today?" he asked instead.

"I've got to pick up a few groceries," Elias replied, scooping batter onto his warm pan. "I was thinking we could go to the St. Lawrence Market?"

Ty made a sound deep in the back of his throat. Elias turned to find him crosseyed, practically drooling onto the table.

"They have the best cheese." He moaned like he was having an orgasm.

Two hours later, knowing parking would be a nightmare late on a Saturday morning, they took the bus from Fort York all the way to The Esplanade, where it was only a two-minute walk to the indoor market.

"Mmmm, cheese," Ty said, heading straight for his favourite cheese shop.

"Get me some, too," Elias said, making his way toward the poultry counter.

"What kind?" Ty was already several feet ahead of him.

"Something good," he said, just to be contrary.

Ty gave him the finger.

"But not Bleu!" he yelled at Ty's retreating back.

Ty waved over his shoulder.

Smiling to himself, he dodged shoppers in his attempt to get to Carnicero's. God, it was packed and much too loud. And why did people bring their kids here? It was so easy for them to get lost in the crowd. Unless they were leashed, like the toddler who ran by him, frazzled mom following behind. Man, that must be so demoralizing. It probably had some kind of negative psychological effect on the kid too. Or maybe not. Did kids remember that sort of humiliation as they grew older?

He shrugged mentally and gritted his teeth as strangers brushed his shoulder, purses and shopping bags bumped his elbow or his legs, strollers blocked half an aisle. Not even noon and the lineups were already ridiculous. Finally reaching the end of Carnicero's' lineup, he was lucky he heard his name called at all in the chaos of disorganized and impatient shoppers.

"Elias!"

There, only a few people up from the front of the line, was Ty's dad, who was waving him over. Elias made his way forward, sending a silent apology to all of the people he bypassed.

"Good thing I saw you," Marty Green said. "It's a fifteen-minute wait from the back of the line."

Four seconds into their conversation, Elias was already looking around for Ty to come save him.

"Ty's around here somewhere," Elias said, just to make conversation with his boyfriend's dad.

Mr. Green waved his words away. "Did he abandon you for the cheese?"

Elias laughed. "He says they have the best here."

"He's not wrong."

The Green siblings had gotten their genetics mostly from their dad: same round chin, same baby face, same ice blue eyes, same blond hair with the dark roots and dark eyebrows. The only thing they'd inherited from their mother was her nose. In Marty Green, Elias could see what Ty would look like in thirty to forty years. Still handsome, with deep laugh lines, strong shoulders, and a full head of hair.

"The wife wants fresh chicken for dinner tonight," Mr. Green said. "But I'm thinking that veal looks good." He stooped to peer into the glass display.

"What can I get you?" one of the attendants asked, a beefy guy in a white chef's coat and red hat.

"Four chicken breasts please, the fresh organic over here," Mr. Green said. Smart move, sticking with what Mrs. Green wanted. Elias couldn't imagine the reaction if Major General Mom didn't get her way. "And whatever my friend's having." By "friend" he meant Elias, if the hand Mr. Green waved in his direction was any indication.

Elias ordered, Ty's dad paid, and they left with their stupidly expensive, fresh organic chicken.

"Thank you," Elias said. "You didn't have to pay."

"My pleasure." Mr. Green gripped Elias's shoulder. "Just make sure my boy eats."

"Oh, trust me, he eats." Elias directed them toward the nearest produce shop then pulled out his phone to text Ty his location. "In fact, we're making chicken fajitas for dinner. Would you and your wife like to join us?"

The surprised pleasure on Mr. Green's face was worth any

nerves Elias might feel about hosting his boyfriend's parents for dinner.

"Thanks, Elias, I'd love that. Let me check with Sue. I'll call Ty later today to confirm, all right?" Mr. Green checked the time on his phone. "Shoot. I've got to head out, pick Maddie up from hockey practice."

"Maddie plays hockey?" That little slip of a girl?

"Goalie." Mr. Green's smile was wide. "She's pretty good. You and Ty should come to one of her games."

Huh, maybe they would.

"Hey, Dad!" Ty appeared at Elias's elbow.

"Hey, kid." Mr. Green gave his son a brief hug. The way they came together with such familiarity and love and belonging formed a lump in Elias's throat. It made him miss the ease with which he'd interacted with his own parents before they died.

"I've got to run and pick up your sister," Mr. Green was telling Ty. "I'll see you tonight. Maybe." He disappeared into the crowd.

"What's happening tonight?" Ty asked.

Elias cleared his throat. "Uh, I may've, uh...invited your parents over for dinner?"

He didn't know what he was expecting from Ty. Disappointment that they wouldn't spend the evening alone together? Embarrassment that Elias had been the one to issue the invite instead of him? Anger that Elias had gone ahead and done so without his consent?

The pleased surprise mirrored the expression on his dad's face so exactly: the raised eyebrows, mouth open in an "O" before his lips twitched at the corners, the half-step backwards. It made Elias laugh.

"Elias?"

He turned. There was Rachel, shopping bags in hand, winter coat open over jeans and a sweater in deference to the market's heat.

"Hi, Rachel."

"I almost didn't recognize you outside of the office," she said, smiling. "Outside of the suits you always wear." She didn't wait for him to respond before gesturing to the tall dark-skinned man next to her. "This is my husband, Aric."

Brief introductions over with, Elias spotted Ty out of the corner of his eye, standing two feet away, looking unsure, bottom lip between his teeth, fingers clenched around the cheese-filled plastic bag in his hands. He looked anywhere but at Elias, as if seeking an escape route or a way to blend into the food stand behind him.

They'd never discussed whether or not they were out at work. Elias wasn't *out*, but he wasn't in the closet either. If someone asked, he wouldn't lie—not that anyone ever asked. Wasn't as if he had any friends other than Rachel at the office anyway. It was hard being a friend when he was also a boss.

For a brief second, he considered ignoring Ty, afraid Rachel might think he was a perv who dated teenagers, but fuck that shit. He couldn't do that to Ty. He felt guilty having the thought, never mind going through with it.

He held out his hand. Ty took it, smile tentative yet thrilled.

"This is my boyfriend, Ty," he said, and he knew how his voice sounded: soft and infatuated, but he couldn't help it. "Ty, this is Rachel, one of my coworkers, and her husband, Aric."

"Oh my gosh! Hi, Ty!" Rachel held out a hand. "It's so nice to meet you."

Aric winced. "Rein it in, woman."

Rachel glared playfully up at her husband before pointing a finger at Elias. "I *knew* you were seeing someone."

"How?" He hadn't done anything different.

"Your resting douchebag face has been more like resting jerk face over the past few weeks."

"And...a jerk isn't as bad as a douchebag?"

"Correct." She nodded once for emphasis.

Ty laughed.

Aric put his arm around his wife and steered her away. "Let's go downstairs. We still need to get the honey."

"Bye, Ty. We should go on a double-date sometime!" Rachel yelled over her shoulder.

"Okay!" Ty grinned and waved at her retreating back.

What the hell just happened?

"My resting douchebag face isn't *that* bad, is it?"

Ty turned, studiously inspecting the red peppers, the lip-biting not doing anything to hide his grin, and didn't answer.

HIS MOM WAS IN LOVE WITH ELIAS. OH, SHE WAS TRYING hard not to show it, but Ty could tell. Her entire focus shifted to him when he talked, she played with her hair, batted her eyes, and she *giggled*. It was so weird. His dad thought it was hilarious.

It wasn't because of anything obvious Elias said or did. It was the little things: how he made sure Ty was served first, how Ty felt comfortable enough in Elias's kitchen to root around the refrigerator for the sour cream when they forgot to put it on the table, how Elias praised Ty's sautéing skills when Ty's mom knew full well that Ty didn't really know what the word meant, how they touched each other subconsciously when they crossed paths in the condo, how they tried to play secret footsies under the dinner table and fooled no one.

She was in love with Elias because Elias was smitten with her son. Damn, Tay felt like a million bucks knowing he was the one putting that smile on Elias's face.

Elias was oblivious, of course, munching away on his fajita, nodding as Ty's mom tried to tell him that the sofa really did belong on the other wall.

Ty licked the salsa off his thumb then gently squeezed Elias's thigh. He was used to his mom trying to take over everything she could. She might be in love with Elias, but it wouldn't stop her from voicing her opinions, wanted or not. Elias was clenched so tightly, he looked ready to explode. Even his knuckles were white on his fajita.

"Mom, how's the planning going for the end-of-season social?" Ty interrupted.

And she was off, complaining about how Maddie's end-of-season hockey social should really be held in the winter since it was a winter sport, but since management *insisted* it be held in early June, they might as well rent some outdoor space and have it outside. Oh, and wouldn't you know? Mrs. Covington's son's friend from school had a brother who worked at the Evergreen Brick Works, who might be able to get them a deal on pricing for their rental space.

Ty tuned her out, glanced at Elias side-eyed. It was obvious to Ty that Elias wasn't paying attention either, just by the way he kept nodding his head.

"Elias," his dad interrupted when his mom paused to take a breath. "Ty says you do some travelling for your photography business. What's been your favourite place you've travelled to so far?"

"The Yukon," Elias said, polishing off his fajita.

Ty had heard this before, so he got up to clear the table, trusting his dad to keep an eye on his mom for him, but she followed him into the kitchen.

"I like that boy," she said, coming up beside him as he rinsed their dinner dishes.

Ty snorted, and even though he didn't need her approval on the guys he dated, it was nice to hear.

"So do I," he said.

"He doesn't seem as sad as when I first met him."

When Ty had moved into his new house, she meant, and Elias had shown up to help. No, Elias wasn't the same as he'd been then. He'd been so distant and lonely then. Ty couldn't reconcile that person with the one laughing with his dad at the kitchen table a few feet away. The one who'd invited Ty's parents for dinner. Who'd called Ty late Wednesday night to tell him he missed him. Who'd texted him at four-thirty in the morning to tell him that it was snowing and did Ty have snow tires? Because if not, Elias could come get him and take him into work. Who Face-Timed with him when they were both watching *Legend of Korra* in their own homes.

"Have you met his family?" his mom asked now, stacking dishes in the dishwasher.

"His parents are both deceased, and his sister lives in Vancouver." It still hurt Ty to think about how alone Elias was.

"It's lucky he has you then," she said.

That was nice to hear, but...

"Why do you say that?" Putting away the sour cream and salsa, he got containers for the leftover chicken and veggies.

"You always see the best in people, Ty, and because of that you bring out the best in them, too. I think Elias needs that, needs someone who sees him for who he is and not the person he shows the world."

Ty blinked at her as she closed the dishwasher and wiped her hands on a dishtowel. Were they even talking about the same thing here?

"Tyler, that chicken's not going to regrow its feet and put itself away."

His mother was *not* a complimenter. She criticized, she complained, she disapproved. Ty and his siblings knew she loved them all, but nothing ever quite lived up to her expectations. To have her say something so nice to him...

"Are you dying?"

Admittedly, it was a stupid question. She'd outlive them all.

"Not until I'm old and grey," she said. "And all of my children have given me grandbabies, including you and Maddison."

Definitely outliving them all.

"Sue, take a look at this," Ty's dad called from the living room. He and Elias were looking at one of Elias's photographs. It hung on the wall between a couple of windows. "We've been here," his dad said to Elias. It was a shot of the Colosseum in Rome, taken from afar and upwards at an angle at night, with the clouds and the moon in the background. It had the same kind of ethereally serene quality his other ones in his second bedroom-cum-office had.

"Oh, yes, I remember." His mom walked over to stand next to his dad. "You and me, no kids."

Ty made a disgusted face behind her back at the image she drew with those five simple words. Elias saw and cleared his throat to cover a laugh.

"I keep telling Ty he should go," his dad said. "He'd love it."

"I'll take him," Elias said.

The way he said it, like it was a given that they'd travel together, like of *course* he'd take Ty... Ty grinned so widely, his cheeks hurt. It meant Elias was thinking long term. They hadn't talked about the future or their relationship, not since that brief conservation on Ty's birthday about going at their own pace. Both of them too afraid to rock the boat, to jinx the good they had going on right now.

"I actually think he might like this better, though," Elias said. He gestured to an image Ty'd fallen in love with when he'd first seen it: a forest in the fall, taken from above, mist dipping between the mountain peaks, the sun bursting through the clouds, painting the green and orange and red treetops in pale yellow light.

His dad grunted. "You're right. He would like that better."

"This is beautiful," his mom breathed. Ty almost fainted at her second compliment of the day. "Where was this taken?"

"Bohemia National Park," Elias replied.

"I'll admit, I don't know where that is. Why don't you work full time for a travel magazine? Your pictures are some of the best I've ever seen."

Ty threw his hands in the air. Hallelujah! Somebody agreed with him. Elias noticed his theatrics and rolled his eyes. Likely he was sick and tired of Ty not-so-subtly trying to convince him that he should take more commissions or become a freelance photographer full time. But swear to God, if Elias mentioned the competitiveness in the photography industry or said, "Seven years at Top Line," one more time, Ty was going to throttle him.

During dessert Ty's mom spent ten minutes telling Elias about the daughter of a friend's cousin whose photography business had crashed because she didn't have a marketing plan. Did Elias have a marketing plan? Did he want the friend's cousin's daughter's phone number so he could talk to her, make sure he didn't make the same mistakes?

"No, thank you," Elias politely declined. "I do pretty well for myself."

They left twenty minutes later with a promise from Ty and Elias that they'd get to one of Maddie's hockey games in the next couple of weeks.

Ty closed to the door behind his parents and leaned back against it, letting out a hard breath.

"Your mom..." Elias said, rubbing his jaw with one hand, brow furrowed.

Ty pointed at him. "Don't blame me! You invited them."

"I was going to say she wasn't that bad tonight."

"She was worse," Ty mumbled, walking himself straight into Elias's arms. Prolonged interaction with his mom always exhausted him, and he nosed his way underneath Elias's collar, breathing in his scent, hoping to banish the fragrance of his mother's perfume from his nostrils. "'Tyler, that chicken's not going to regrow its feet and put itself away,'" he mimicked in his mom's voice.

Elias laughed. "I didn't know your mom was funny."

Ty groaned. "Oh no, I've created a monster."

Elias laughed harder. Ty clung to him tighter, the vibrations of Elias's chest against his as he laughed soothing and comforting.

"Would you really take me to Rome?" Ty asked, pulling back a touch to commit Elias's smile to memory.

"I'd take you anywhere you want."

"Can we start with the bedroom?" Ty asked, mouth millimeters away from Elias's.

Elias's eyes heated, hands tightening on Ty's lower back. "We can definitely start with the bedroom."

Chapter Ten

If you've been in a slump lately, Capricorn, don't worry—this week's an excellent one to start making those changes you've secretly been dreaming about.

"You!"

As Elias had expected, Rachel strode into his office Monday morning before he'd even booted up his computer.

"I have a bone to pick with you. I can't *believe* you didn't tell me you have a boyfriend."

Yup, almost word-for-word what'd he expected her to say.

She stood there in dark pants and a purple blouse, hands fisted on her hips with a look on her face that could only be described as an annoyed glower. An annoyed glower that quickly turned into a pout.

"I thought we were friends," she said, dropping into his visitor's chair.

Were they? Were they friends? He'd always considered them work friends, the type who only chatted within office confines and didn't really tell each other anything about themselves except inconsequential surface stuff like what area of the city they lived in, where'd they'd gone to school, and where they were from, figuring Rachel wouldn't want to be friends with him outside of work.

Had he made a mistake? They did text on the weekends after all, though those conversations were strictly about his horoscope. Yet she had mentioned double dating.

"Tell me everything," Rachel said. "Have you met his

family? Are they good people? What's Ty like? Do you have a lot in common? What does he do?"

Elias's head swam from all the questions, and for some reason, the only one he could really focus on was that last one.

"Uh, he works for the city," he dodged.

"Like in politics?"

Shit, that was so far from the truth, it was laughable. "No, he works in waste management."

"Cool, doing what?"

He didn't want to tell her that Ty was a garbage man. He also didn't want to reflect too deeply on *why* he didn't want to tell her, certain he'd come out the other end of that looking like a self-absorbed douchebag who was embarrassed of his own boyfriend. Because he didn't want to analyze himself anymore—and Rachel was still waiting for an answer—he said, "I can't remember exactly."

"I can't wait to get to know him!"

Rachel and Ty? Oh God, they'd get into all sorts of trouble. The thought scared him a little, so he blurted, "Change."

Rachel blinked at him. "Huh?"

Elias cleared his throat. "Uh, my daily horoscope?"

"Oh!" she said, as if she'd forgotten about the conversation they'd been having every morning for the past eight months, ever since Rachel started studying what she called "spiritual stuff": horoscopes and moon phases and guardian angels and crystals and tarot and reiki—whatever reiki was.

"What did it say?" she asked.

"Just that this is a good week for change."

"Huh. And do you want anything to change?"

He looked away but not before he saw her crinkled brow and narrowed eyes. She was peering at him as though she was only just realizing that she didn't really know him, and she'd be right. And that was mostly his fault, wasn't it? He'd known

Ty for four weeks and he could say with confidence that Ty knew him better than anybody else on the planet even though he and Rachel had been working together for the past three years.

What did that say about him? Kevin—his best friend in Ireland—often told him that he was guarded and aloof to the point of unfriendliness, but Ty... Something about him, about the way they were so in sync with each other, had Elias letting him in much faster than anyone else who came before him.

Sometimes he missed the simplicity of those first few days with Ty, when he could ply Ty with I'm-sorry beverages and pastries and not have to make himself vulnerable to another person. But what they had now was much more than a hook-up, more than dating... It was a full-fledged relationship with all the bells and whistles that came with it, including dinner with the—dare he say it—in-laws.

And he wanted to keep Ty, forever if Ty would have him. Maybe it was too soon to be thinking that way after, but he didn't care. They'd decided to go at their own pace, and if Elias's pace was firmly set to recklessly-fast, then sue him. Besides he had a feeling that Ty was in the same place.

He was saved from having to answer Rachel when his phone pinged. Picking it up, he glanced at the email notification before waving the phone at her.

"I need to answer this."

"Sure."

She rose slowly, eyes still narrowed, like he was a puzzle she was trying to figure out. He sighed when she finally took herself out of his office, but his relief was short-lived. She poked her head back in.

"You should invite Ty to Julie's retirement party next Friday," she said.

He didn't even want to go to Julie's retirement party, never mind subjecting Ty to it. The only reason he was going was because Julie was the current VP and a Top Line lifer. They'd worked closely together for the past seven years, and it was her job Elias was angling for. Although maybe if he invited Ty, he wouldn't be so damn bored and ill at ease.

"Yeah, maybe," he said, but Rachel was already gone.

Double-tapping the email notification on his phone, he brought up the message—a personal one, not work-related like he'd led Rachel to believe. Shit. It'd been three weeks since the HR reps at *CanadaTravels* had emailed him about their open Director of Photography position, and he'd completely forgotten to respond.

Dear Mr. Hood,

I hope this email finds you well. I'm following up on my last email dated 15 January. As previously mentioned, we'd love to speak with you about the open position of Director of Photography at CanadaTravels. *Martha Lloyd speaks very highly of you and your work. Please see the attached document for a description of the position and salary. I hope to hear from you at your earliest convenience.*

Man. They still hadn't filled that role? There had to be hundreds of people equally qualified as him.

Elias hit reply, but his fingers wouldn't type out the message he'd composed in his head, one that sounded vaguely like "Thank you for the offer, but I'm very happy at my current place of employment." That "very happy" didn't sound genuine even to him. And he could hear Ty's words in his head, picking at him like a hungry bird, telling him how talented he was and that he was wasting his time at Top Line, sitting on his ass as he waited for his life to start.

Okay, in fairness to Ty, he'd never told Elias that he was wasting his time. That thought was all Elias, who in some tiny, dark corner of his mind had trouble acknowledging that Ty was right. Maybe he should take more commissions. Maybe he should go freelance full time... But that prospect had the breath backing up in his lungs. No steady income? Hell no.

But this Director of Photography position... Except for the decrease in salary, it hit all of his buttons. Taking pictures? Check. Getting to use his under-utilized creative skills? Check. Working for a company he admired? Check. In a capacity he was comfortable and semi-experienced in? Check. A little bit of travelling? Check. A close-knit working environment? Check. Finally putting his minor in photography to good use? Check.

Elias's forehead hit his desk. He couldn't do it, couldn't write that thank-you-but-no-thank-you email. What had his horoscope said again, about making changes secretly dreamt about? And yet the thought of leaving Top Line and starting something new knotted his chest.

Fuck, he was a mess.

Chapter Eleven

IT WAS AN ACCIDENT. TY DIDN'T MEAN TO SNOOP, BUT when the ping sounded, he checked the phones on Elias's kitchen island to see who'd received the email. Wasn't him, so he checked Elias's phone to make sure it wasn't anything urgent.

And holy jumping cheese crackers, Batman! He gasped at the subject line and almost choked on his Shreddies—dinner of champions. Holy shit, holy shit, holy shit! It was from someone named Martha Lloyd.

Subject: Director of Photography

Hey Elias,

Would you have time this week to meet with me so we can discuss the Director of Photography position with...

That was it. Stupid tiny notification box. With *who*, damn it? Who was the position with? Gritting his teeth against the urge to double-tap and bring up the full email, he stuffed his face with his last bite of cereal and flipped the phone upside down on the countertop to curb temptation. But as he washed his bowl and spoon, he kept one eye on the phone as if it would give up its secrets by virtue of him staring metaphorical daggers at it.

"You ready?" Elias came into the kitchen dressed down in dark jeans and a long-sleeved Henley. Why did he always have to look like a damn fashion model? Ty's own jeans, loose T, and flannel shirt were clean and comfy, but he looked like a chump in comparison to Elias. Ah well. He was who he was.

"Should I change?" Elias asked, gaze raking Ty up and down. Ty couldn't deny that Elias's dark brown elevator look

—starting at Ty's thick-socked feet and travelling upward to his chest then roaming back down again—made his dick stir in his pants, even though the look was more information-gathering and less sexy-playtime.

"I should change," Elias answered his own question. "I'm too fancy for a hockey game."

"You're fine," Ty said. He cleared his throat to get rid of the gravel. "Better than fine, in fact. Definitely don't change."

Elias was smirking at him—yeah, the man knew he was hot, and he knew Ty thought he was off-the-charts sexy. Ty rolled his eyes, brushed Elias's cheek with a quick kiss and walked out of the kitchen.

"Just gotta brush my teeth," he called over his shoulder. "Your phone's on the island."

Maybe Elias would look at it and see the email. Maybe he'd see it and read it. Maybe he'd read it and then tell Ty all about it. Director of Photography? Ty didn't really know what that entailed exactly, but it sounded right up Elias's alley.

He couldn't stop grinning as he brushed his teeth, which, it turned out, made it doubly hard to brush said teeth. He was still grinning when he headed back to Elias, waiting in the front entrance, clad in his wool coat and winter boots. Ty bit his lip to hide a grin. It didn't work, if Elias's bewildered smile was anything to go by.

"What are you smiling at?"

I saw the email from Martha Lloyd, and I can't believe you applied for a photography position and didn't tell me about it! But I don't even care about that because OH MY GOD! Director of Photography!

Things not to say because one, it would steal Elias's thunder, and two, Elias would know he'd been snooping. Inadvertently snooping, but it was still snooping.

Instead Ty said, "Nothing. Just thinking you should be in front of the camera instead of behind it."

Elias snorted and held Ty's jacket out to him. "Not in this lifetime."

They were halfway out the door when Ty said, "You got your phone?"

"Yeah." Elias drew the word out, stretching it to five syllables, eyes narrowed on Ty. Likely because Ty was always on him about how much time he spent on his phone, answering work emails—like many corporate nine-to-fivers, Elias brought his work home and Ty hated it—and was now probably wondering what the fuck was wrong with him.

"In case we get separated," Ty hastily explained and headed for the elevators.

Elias didn't mention anything about the email on the walk to the building's parking garage. He didn't mention it on the drive to the Larry Grossman Memorial Arena in Toronto's Forest Hill neighbourhood. Nothing during the brief walk from the parking lot to the arena.

But okay, that was fine. It probably meant that Elias had yet to check his phone, which made no sense. Elias was annoyingly glued to the damn thing, but it was a possibility. Or Elias had read the email, but he was still processing its contents. That particular scenario was much more likely. Elias was a thinker. He'd have to mull over what the email said and how he felt about it and whether or not he wanted to act on it and how it would affect him if he did and build out a mental pros and cons list. Basically, he'd analyze it to death before mentioning it to Ty, but that was fine. Elias could analyze to his heart's content as long as he took the damn job. He'd tell Ty eventually. Ty just needed to be patient.

"Are you okay?" Elias asked as they walked through the arena doors.

"Yeah. Why?"

"You were very fidgety on the drive here."

Crap. His giddiness at Elias's maybe new job was showing. "I'm fine," he insisted.

"Maybe no more Shreddies for dinner," Elias suggested.

Ty laughed and laughed, even though he had no idea why he found that so funny. He was just in a damn good mood.

"Definitely no more Shreddies," Elias muttered, eyes going comically wide when Ty continued to cackle.

"Elias!" A yell from the ice rink's stands.

His entire family was here, not just his parents and siblings. There was also his in-laws and all of his nieces and nephews. He'd never seen this many people at one of Maddie's hockey games. Did nobody have anything better to do on a Tuesday night in February? Not that he should judge. He was here too, wasn't he?

"Man, I'm glad you're here," Jeremy said to Elias when he and Ty approached the Green posse, clumped together in a group. "I'm travelling to Boston next week for work. Ty mentioned you travel a lot, so I was wondering if you've ever been to Boston? Can you give me some tips on what to see and do and where to eat? Oh, hey Ty."

Ty snorted a laugh, not at all offended that his brother was ignoring him in favour of talking to Elias. In fact, he loved that half of his family greeted Elias first. Loved the kiss on the cheek Elias gave Ty's mom. Loved the shy smile Elias got from Ty's niece, Hannah. Loved the, "Hey, dude!" shot Elias's way from Matt. Loved how Elias sat between Jeremy and Jenn—which was about four people away from where Ty sat next to his dad—and that he felt comfortable doing so.

Loved him. Just loved him. It was that simple. And when Elias winked at Hannah when the five-year-old turned to smile at him again, Ty was done. Stick a fork in him, he was done. Every single part of him was Elias's, begging to be loved and held and wanted by the man for the rest of his life. It made him feel funny, as if his heart contained every possible good feeling in the world, about to burst like a popped balloon into heart-shaped confetti at Elias's feet, where Elias could either scoop them up so they didn't get stepped on and broken, or let them scatter into the wind.

Ty was banking on that first option, because he had a feeling that Elias felt the same, or was on his way to feeling the same. And for now, that was just as good.

BY FRIDAY ELIAS STILL HADN'T SHARED ANYTHING ABOUT the email, and Ty was sick of waiting.

But he was also lying on his stomach on his bed, thoroughly blissed-out and satisfied, trying to stay awake after a mind-numbing orgasm that stole any desire to move.

Elias nuzzled his temple, beard scritching against his skin. "Don't fall asleep on me," he said, voice rumbly.

"Okay," Ty said, reaching out blindly to pat Elias's chest, having no intention of complying. He could already feel himself drifting into sleep.

"Ty." Elias kissed his nose. "Ty." Cheek. "Ty." Shoulder.

Ty couldn't help but laugh. "What?"

"Stay awake."

"Why?"

"Because I'm hungry and you don't have any food."

The pout in Elias's voice had Ty finally opening his eyes to take a good look at him. His boyfriend looked charmingly petulant.

"Well, yeah. I've been at your place all week," Ty said. "I told you we should've stopped at the store before coming here."

"But I couldn't fuck you in a grocery store," Elias explained. "There's nowhere for you to fall asleep after."

Ty laughed, remembering how handsy Elias had been on

the drive from his condo to Ty's house in Puslinch. How Elias had talked dirty the whole time, describing how he was going to get Ty home and naked and stretched out underneath him, where he'd proceed to drive him crazy with his mouth and hands before he fucked him into the mattress.

And four seconds after walking in the door, he'd done exactly that. The memory had Ty's dick coming to life.

"I have cereal," he offered.

"Cereal's not dinner food," Elias protested, flopping onto his back.

Ty crawled closer and stretched himself out against Elias's gloriously cut brown body, head on his shoulder. Elias's arm came around him, hand squeezing his ass. Ty's newly awakened cock poked Elias in the hip.

"Cereal's the best kind of dinner food," Ty argued.

Elias sighed deeply in what sounded more like satisfaction —their naked bodies were plastered together, after all—and less like acquiescence on the cereal issue. "Fine," he said. "But not Shreddies. Those made you loopy."

Chuckling, Ty snuggled closer, Elias's arm tightening around him. The man might be hungry, but he made no move to get up. Ty took advantage and ran one hand over Elias's defined abs, tracing the ridges under his fingers. Not to stimulate or jumpstart a second round; just to touch, to feel Elias breathe. To feel closer to him.

He didn't want to think that Elias was purposely hiding from him, but the fact that he hadn't talked to him about that email yet was troubling. He knew Elias, knew Elias would think it through until his brain started to hurt before he talked to anyone about it, but Ty liked to think he was different. They were a team. Hopefully Elias would discuss any major life changes with him, just like Ty had discussed the junior waste management position with the city of Guelph with him.

But he didn't like that he'd seen the email, and Elias didn't know he'd seen it. It made him feel guilty, like he was spying, even though it really wasn't his fault, and he didn't like having that between them.

Okay, it was maybe a little bit his fault.

Lifting up and propping his head on his hand, he bit his lip uncertainly before blurting, "Don't get mad."

The expression that crossed Elias's face was a mix of anxious and amused: narrowed eyes and a furrowed brow combined with lips titled into a half-smile. "That's not a great way to start a conversation."

Heaving himself up, Ty sat cross-legged on the bed next to Elias. He couldn't have a conversation with most of his body touching Elias's. It was too distracting.

"Is this a serious conversation?" Elias asked before Ty could continue.

"Um...yes?"

"Okay."

When Elias swung his legs over the side of the bed and got up, Ty's heart jumped into his throat before he realized Elias wasn't leaving. He slipped on his briefs and handed Ty his boxers.

"I can't have a serious conversation while naked," Elias explained. "Not with your dick staring me in the face."

Ty glanced down. Said dick was no longer semi-hard, probably because this conversation scared Ty a little, forcing a quick retreat from his dick. Rolling his eyes at himself, he put on his boxers as Elias sat across from him.

"What's going on?" Elias said.

Ty cleared his throat and played with a loose thread in his bedcover. "You remember on Tuesday, before Maddie's game? I was sitting in the kitchen eating dinner? Well, you got an email on your phone, and I checked it to make sure it wasn't anything urgent..."

"Okay," Elias said, clearly confused.

Ty forced himself to meet his gaze. "I saw it. The email, I mean. I didn't mean to, I swear! I just wanted to make sure it wasn't something you had to deal with right away."

Elias shrugged. "Okay," he said again.

Ty blinked. "Okay?"

"Yeah." Elias's smile turned amused and relieved, as if he'd expected worse news. "You were only trying to help, right?"

"Right. Of course." Ty continued to blink at him. Waited for Elias to explain about the email. When nothing came, Ty said, "So what did you do about it?"

"About what?"

Was Elias being dense on purpose? "About the email." What else?

"Which email was it, baby? I get a lot of emails in one day, so you'll have to be more specific."

Light dawned. Of *course,* Elias wasn't upset he'd seen his email. Elias didn't even know *which* email he was referring to. He probably thought he'd seen some innocuous inter-office email about a potluck or next week's retirement party for the VP Elias had invited him to.

"Um..." Ty hesitated, because if anything was going to rock their comfortable boat, it was probably this—Elias's job. "It was from Martha Lloyd. Something about a Director of Photography position?"

Elias's face blanked before Ty finished speaking. That didn't bode well.

"Oh."

Elias looked out the window, but since it was dark out and they had the light on inside, it bounced their wavery reflections back at them. He ran a hand through his hair. Ty waited some more.

"Okay."

Jesus, it was like pulling fucking teeth!

"That's all you have to say?" Ty asked. He knew his voice was incredulous, but he couldn't help himself. "*Okay?* Can you at least tell me... Who's Martha? Did you ever meet with her? Did you talk about the job? What *is* the job exactly? Who's it with? Did you take it?"

Elias snorted a darkly amused laugh. With an eyebrow raised he asked, "Anything else you want to know?"

Ty was not amused. This was huge! How could Elias sit there and act as if it wasn't a big deal?

"I... What did you... Are you...?" Ugh! He was so ticked off at the way Elias was treating his new job opportunity that the words backed up in his throat, threatening to choke him.

Taking pity on him, Elias took one of Ty's hands in both of his. "Martha and I went to Queen's together, and we worked on the school newspaper at the same time. We've kept in touch sporadically over the past ten years. She's the creative director at *CanadaTravels*, and she's been trying to bring me on as Director of Photography for the past few months. They've been having trouble finding somebody who fits, and she's convinced I'm the person for the job."

He goddamn *was* the person for the job. Holy crap! This was amazing!

But wait...

"For the past few months?" Ty said. "That means...you've been turning her down for *months*?"

It was official: His boyfriend was crazy.

"Did you at least meet with her like she asked?"

Elias nodded. "We met yesterday."

"That's great! And?"

He briefed Ty on the job, and the more he talked, the more Ty's eyes widened. Working with the art, editorial, and digital teams to come up with creative magazine concepts? Scheduling photo shoots and coordinating with freelance photographers? Occasional travel to take pictures himself?

Overseeing staff? Tweaking images? Directing photo and video shoots?

It was all right up his alley. Ty grinned from ear to ear, but the best thing was, so was Elias. He was so clearly excited about this opportunity, yet Ty couldn't help the sinking feeling in his gut.

"Did you take the job?" he interrupted Elias to ask, already knowing the answer.

Elias hesitated. Ty's heart sank.

"Ty, I'm *this* close—" Elias held his thumb and forefinger a centimetre apart. "—to getting the VP job at Top Line, and I've been with them for seven years, and—"

Ty groaned and fell back on the bed, rubbing his eyes with his palms. There it was again. That damn "seven years at Top Line" excuse. Why was that a good reason for Elias to stay in a job he hated?

He didn't realize he was mumbling under his breath, until Elias said, "Why are you mad?"

He was mad because his stupid, stubborn boyfriend couldn't see the opportunity dangling in front of his face with bright, neon Broadway lights! But he couldn't bring emotion into this conversation, not with Elias, Mr. Must Remain Calm and Logical Lest Anybody Realize I Have Actual Feelings. Ty took a deep breath and sat back up.

"Do you remember last weekend, when I applied for the Guelph job? You told me that maybe the reason I got hired with the city of Toronto was so that I could meet my current supervisor, who would recommend me for the job? Like it was all meant to happen this way?"

Elias nodded, though he didn't appear to have any clue where Ty was going with this train of thought.

"Maybe," Ty continued, "the fact that Martha and *Canada-Travels* have been trying to get you on board for the last few months is a sign that you're meant to make this change."

The skepticism on Elias's face wasn't unexpected, but still...

"Really?" Ty threw his hands in the air, unable to keep his emotions contained anymore. Screw Elias and his self-controlled detachment. "Why did that argument work when you said it, but not when I do?"

"Ty, it's not that." Elias took his hand again. "Don't get mad at me when I say this, okay? But seven years at Top Line —" Ty gritted his teeth. Elias squeezed his hand. "—means seven years of experience, seven years at the same organization, where I know what I'm doing and where I know all the players, where I've worked my way up, where everything is familiar, where I'm respected. To go from that to *Canada-Travels* where I'd be the new guy again, not knowing anything or anyone, having to start from scratch... It's..."

Scary was what it was. Ty was sort of going through the same thing.

As if he'd read Ty's mind, Elias continued. "You understand, right? I mean, you have an interview on Monday for the Guelph job. You've got to be at least a little anxious about starting somewhere new?"

The fight went out of Ty. Yeah, he understood exactly the dilemma Elias was facing. Sometimes sticking with the familiar was easier than making a change, even when a change might make your life better.

"I get it," Ty said. "I do. The difference is I like my job. You don't."

Elias avoided his gaze. "Why do you say that?"

"Because when you were listing the reasons for staying with Top Line, not once did you say 'I like my job.' You never do."

A ragged sigh from Elias. He closed his eyes and swallowed hard, clearly rattled by Ty's words, as if maybe it was something he'd considered before but hadn't wanted to admit to himself. Ty's heart went out to him. He gave Elias's hand a squeeze.

"I just want you to be happy," he rasped.

"Ty." Elias's eyes caught his, the honesty and sincerity in them making it impossible for Ty to look away even if he'd wanted to. "I'm the happiest I've ever been," he whispered. "And that's because of you."

His heart was in his eyes, and Ty's breath caught at the love he saw there. The wonder he felt every time Elias opened up to him made him smile tremulously, and he scooted forward until their knees bumped. Elias might not be the best at expressing himself, but he knew how to make his words count when he did.

Ty glanced down at his hand, still clutched in both of Elias's. His own winter-light skin and Elias's light brown—a combination, Elias had once said, of his biological parents: a Middle Eastern mother and Scottish father. Ty loved how their skin slid together, how they looked next to each other, a contrast, light and dark, like the sky at noon versus twilight.

"Is it, um..." Ty had to pause to clear the lump from his throat. Not wanting to miss Elias's reaction, he met his gaze. "Is it too soon to tell you I love you?"

Not if the smile on Elias's face was anything to go by. Elias pulled on Ty's hand. "Come here."

Ty went, straddling Elias's lap and burying his face in his neck. He squeezed tight, and was squeezed so tightly back he thought he could just stay cocooned in Elias's warmth and strength forever.

"I love you," Elias whispered into Ty's shoulder. Ty grinned hugely and laughed against Elias's neck. "What's funny?"

Ty shook his head. "Just happy."

"Happy enough to find me some food?" Elias's stomach rumbled as he asked. "Because fuck, I'm starving."

Ty hadn't been home since last week, and he tried to mentally catalogue what he had in his pantry besides cereal. He stifled a laugh when he realized...

"I think I only have Shreddies."

"Oh, good God," Elias said through a groan.

"But there's no milk." Ty delivered the news with all of the end-of-the-world somberness he could find.

"Are you kidding me?" Elias huffed.

Ty gave up the ghost and laughed his ass off all the way downstairs.

Chapter Twelve

Happy Valentine's Day, Capricorn! If you don't have anyone special to celebrate with this year, not to worry: Venus is still visible to the naked eye for the next few days. Take advantage of the planet of love's energy and influence.

Everything was perfect. So perfect, in fact, that Elias kept holding his breath and tried to ignore that feeling of trepidation in his chest that signalled impending doom.

Ever since Elias had surprised Ty with a visit on his birthday in mid-January—God, he still couldn't believe he'd done that—they'd been living out of each other's pockets. They spent the work week at Elias's, since they both worked downtown, and as a bonus, Ty didn't have to get up for work as early. Weekends were spent either at Elias's condo or at Ty's home in Puslinch.

They shared the grocery bill, fought over the last of the Saturday morning pancakes, kept clothes and toiletries at each other's places, continued to meet for coffee and hot chocolate every morning before Elias went to work, had each other's friends and family's contact information in their phones. In Ty's case he only had Kevin, whom Elias had introduced him to over video call a couple of weeks ago.

Things couldn't be better. Which meant they couldn't last. Nothing ever did. But he wasn't going to think about that tonight.

Elias powered down his computer and placed a couple of folders in his messenger bag. Took them back out. Fuck it, he removed his cell phone and house keys and put them in his coat pocket, planning to leave his entire bag at the office for once. It was Valentine's Day for fuck's sake. Ty was likely already waiting for him at home—probably napping on the couch. It wasn't like Elias was going to get any work done tonight.

He was waiting for the elevator—an hour early, but whatever—grocery bag in one hand, gift bag in the other, when Julie, the retiring VP, caught up to him, her soft-soled shoes noiseless on the linoleum.

"Elias, there you are." He'd recognize that British accent anywhere. "Do you have a few minutes to meet with John and me before you leave?"

Did he have time to meet with the VP as well as the president & CEO? Yeah, he had time. Although a little curl of resentment tightened his smile as he sat on the sofa in John's spacious office, Julie next to him and John seated on an office chair across from him. They were cutting into his time with Ty.

Julie and John couldn't have been more mismatched if they'd tried. John was dressed down in jeans and a checkered shirt—which meant he probably didn't have any meetings today—his white hair sticking up in every direction. Julie's plaid skirt and jacket, on the other hand, looked like they came from Medieval Scotland.

"Elias, thank you for joining us," said John. "Looks like you were on your way out. Sorry about that. This won't take long."

"It's fine. I'm not in a rush," he lied.

"We wanted to speak with you about the VP position," Julie said.

Elias held his breath.

"As you know we've been reviewing applications since Thanksgiving," John said. "Yours has always been at the top of the pile. You've been with us for a long time, you know the organization, how we work, and your staff speak extremely highly of you."

It felt a little bit like John was buttering him up only to let him down gently, so to say he was shocked when John said, "The job's yours," was a bit of an understatement.

"I'm sorry, what?"

John chuckled at his reaction.

"We're offering you the job," Julie said.

"You don't have to decide right this second," John said, smiling at the perplexed look Elias was sure was on his face. "We understand that it's a big decision. The job is more... everything. More travelling, more responsibility, more staff management, more damage control, more consulting, more money."

The VP position... It was *his*? Why was he having such a hard time wrapping his mind around that? It was everything he'd ever wanted, right at his fingertips.

Then why did it leave him feeling hollow?

"It'd be great if you could let us know by Friday morning." Julie picked up a resume from the coffee table and handed it to him. "We'd like to announce it at my retirement party on Friday evening, and if you don't take the job, this is who we plan to hire for it. We wanted to let you know whom you'd be reporting to, if you decide to stay in your current position."

Too overwhelmed by what was happening, Elias couldn't focus on the words on the page. Whoever the person on this resume was, John and Julie's backup person if Elias didn't accept the position, he was sure he or she would be an excellent fit. Top Line didn't hire amateurs. He had two days—less than that, more like forty hours—to let them know if he wanted the VP job...the one he'd been hoping for for months.

But he didn't need those forty hours. He already knew what his answer was.

Chapter Thirteen

Elias was right: Ty was napping on the couch when he walked in the door almost an hour and a half later. Setting down his bags, he divested himself of his boots and coat and shucked his suit jacket, leaving it draped over one of the kitchen island's stools.

Dressed in boxers and a hoodie, Ty lay on his back on the couch, one arm flung over his head. The other rested on his stomach, thumb hooked into a book, marking the page he'd left off at before passing out. Elias set it face down on the coffee table so Ty didn't lose his page, then laid himself gently over Ty. Lining up their bodies perfectly, he pressed tiny kisses to his boyfriend's face. It only took seconds for Ty to wake since he never slept too deeply or too long during his after-work naps.

Lifting his arms, Ty wrapped them around Elias's neck and pulled until Elias's entire weight was on him in a full-body hug.

"Hi, baby," Elias mumbled into Ty's neck. He was warm and scruffy and smelled like the pine-scented soap he kept in Elias's bathroom. Ty grumbled a sleepy greeting in return and spread his legs so Elias could settle between them. A just-woke-up Ty was always cuddly and cute. Elias nuzzled his neck. Ty squirmed and huffed a laugh.

"What?"

"Your beard tickles," Ty said, voice sleep-rough.

Elias grunted. Lifting his head, he smiled at Ty. "Should I shave it?"

Ty cupped his face in both hands, running his palms over

his beard. "Never." He brought Elias's face down for a kiss. Elias went willingly, licking his way into Ty's mouth, tongues tangling together. Ty tasted slightly minty, like he'd brushed his teeth before conking out. He hardened against Elias's thigh, which made his own dick stir in his pants. It never took more than a few seconds for Ty to get him all fired up. He hoped it never changed, even if sometimes it happened at inappropriate moments—like when Ty licked his fingers clean after sampling something at the grocery store.

"Wait," Elias said, pulling back, stopping things before they went too far.

Ty raised an eyebrow. "*Wait*? Not a word I thought you'd ever say under these conditions."

Elias chuckled and sat up. Grasping Ty's hand, he yanked him to a seated position next to him.

"There's something I need to talk to you about," Elias said.

"Does it involve the chocolate syrup I bought today?" Ty's smile was wicked and lascivious.

"Did you?" Elias toed off his socks. "I bought some too."

"*Extra* syrup?"

Ty got that look in his eyes Elias knew meant nothing good, so he distracted him before he could get too many thoughts in his head about what to do with extra chocolate syrup.

"I got the VP job."

The expression on Ty's face was tough to describe. A weird mixture of disappointment, anxiety, and happiness flitted over his features before his lips curved in a smile that, while it wasn't quite forced, lacked its usual wattage.

"Oh, wow. Congratulations, Eli." His smile transformed into something much more genuine as he said the words, and it hit Elias that even though Ty didn't particularly care for what Elias did for a living, he was sincerely happy that Elias had gotten what he wanted. Elias was so humbled by that thought and by Ty's generosity that he cupped Ty's neck and hauled him for a kiss that scorched his insides and left them both panting.

When he let Ty's mouth go, he said, "I turned it down."

"Huh?" Ty was wonderfully dazed, his mouth curved in a shy smile Elias rarely saw.

"I turned it down."

"You... Wait, what?" Ty shook his head. "You turned it down?" He said it slowly, clearly still trying to understand.

"I turned it down," Elias confirmed for a third time.

"You turned down...the VP position...that you've wanted for months?"

"Correct. Also, I quit. Gave my two weeks notice."

Ty's face blanked. "Who the fuck are you right now?"

Elias laughed so hard he had to hold his stomach. He'd never felt so free.

Ty straddled his lap and cupped his face, peering into his eyes with his own narrowed ones. "Oh God, he's gone mental," he muttered. "Completely bonkers."

Elias kept chuckling. "Oh, and also?"

Ty looked like he physically braced himself for Elias's third bit of news.

"I took the Director of Photography job."

No reaction from Ty. Until seconds later, when the words finally sunk in. His eyes went anime-wide, mouth stretching into the biggest grin Elias had ever seen. He brought his hands to his mouth, looking like a five-year-old given a puppy for Christmas. Then he launched himself at Elias, making a high-pitched "Eeeeee" sound that had Elias wincing.

"Oh my God!" he yelled in Elias's year. "Really? Really?" He pulled back to look at Elias, who nodded. "Oh my God! Oh my God." His voice went from happiness to wonder. "We both got new jobs today."

They'd *both* gotten...? "Baby, did you get the position in Guelph?"

Ty nodded. "I was going to text you about it, but I didn't want to bother you at work."

"Ty." Elias waited for him to meet his eyes. "You can bother me as much as you want, okay? I like hearing from you throughout the day." He was rewarded with another shy smile. "Especially when it's for something like this. Congrats, baby. I'm proud of you."

But the smile had slipped off Ty's face.

"What's wrong?" Elias asked.

"I just realized we won't see each other as much anymore since I won't be working in the city."

"I won't either," Elias said.

Ty's eyebrows winged up. "You won't?"

"Nope. *CanadaTravels*'s offices are in Hamilton of all places."

"Oh, well that's good for you. You'll be commuting against traffic."

"Yeah, for a while, until I move closer."

"You're not going to stay here?"

"No," Elias said. "I'd rather sell this place and move than have a long commute. Want to help me start looking for a place this weekend? I was thinking Oakville or Burlington, maybe Stoney Creek."

Ty bit his lip, fiddling with Elias's shirt buttons. Elias rubbed his hands up and down Ty's lightly-haired thighs, waiting him out, knowing that whatever Ty had on his mind, he'd spit it out in a minute. Sometimes he just needed a few seconds to sort the thoughts out in his head and properly word whatever it was he wanted to say.

"Do you want to maybe...move in with me?" Ty's eyes met his before shifting quickly away.

Move in with Ty, into his charming home in the country?

Share the bills and a mortgage and a bathroom and a drive-way? More importantly, share a home and a life? Elias could picture it so easily: a house that smelled like Ty's hot choco-late, the two of them cooking dinner together in Ty's seven-ties-style kitchen, sharing chores, growing old together, maybe getting a dog they could walk together before and after work—something cute and fuzzy Ty would name Puff or Snowshoe or Waffles or something equally as fun. God, he wanted that so bad his stomach flipped.

"Yes."

A frown marred Ty's boyish face. "Yes?"

"Yes." Elias grinned at his shocked face. "Did you want me to say no?"

"No!" Ty leaned down and rested his forehead against Elias's. "I just thought I'd have to convince you."

"Did the convincing involve the chocolate syrup?" Elias was done talking. His hands slid from Ty's thighs, up over his hips, and ended on his ass, where he cupped and squeezed, kneading the firm globes. Fuck, he loved the way Ty instantly responded with a whimper and a ragged release of breath.

"It definitely involved the chocolate syrup," Ty murmured, voice gone husky. He ground his growing erection against Elias's. "And an orgasm or four."

"Four?" Elias lifted his head, his lips a hair's breadth away from Ty's. "Ambitious."

"Not really. Just horny," Ty admitted before he closed the tiny gap between them.

This kiss? It was on a completely different scale of smutty than the lazy one they'd shared earlier after Elias had woken Ty up. It was an inferno about to burn them both alive, each of them pulling at the other's clothes, breaths hitching when their erections bumped, groans and expletives following roaming hands.

"Need you," Ty said against Elias's throat. "Right now."

Elias heaved himself off the couch, Ty wrapped around him like a clinging monkey, leaving their discarded clothing in the living room. He fell on top of Ty after setting him down on the bed, but Ty was having none of it. He quickly flipped them over. Elias landed on his back with a muttered, "Oof," Ty's naked body on top of him. Lips landed on his nipple, and Elias groaned at the slight bite of pain when Ty used his teeth, electricity pooling in his gut.

Fuck the foreplay, Elias wanted Ty inside him, and he wanted it now. Reaching over into the night table, he blindly felt for the lube and condoms and tossed them on the bed.

Ty grinned. "In a hurry?"

He was teasing, but Elias was dead serious when he said, "Yes. Fuck me."

Ty's entire body stopped moving, lips just above Elias's belly button, hand wrapped around Elias's dick. Elias could feel him vibrating above him.

"Really?" Ty's voice was gravel, and he blinked owlishly at Elias. So far, Elias had always topped, but today he needed Ty.

Elias only grinned at him.

"Fuck, you're so hot." Ty crawled back up Elias's body and kissed him hotly, wetly, grinding his erection down on Elias's. The feel of Ty above him just made Elias more desperate to have that hard dick inside him.

Grabbing the lube, Ty must've read his mind, because he didn't waste any time slicking up his fingers and probing at Elias's hole. Elias spread his legs as wide as he could to make it easier for him, and yet he couldn't help the flare of apprehension that briefly paralyzed his muscles when Ty inserted a finger into him and his whole body tensed with nerves.

"Easy," Ty whispered, using his free hand to massage Elias's inner thigh. His tongue licked a path up the underside of Elias's erection, over the prominent vein there. Licks of heat winging up and down his spine, Elias was so turned on by the hot licks and the thigh massage that he didn't realize Ty had inserted a second finger until he scissored them apart, stretching Elias. When he was satisfied with that, he did something with his fingers, hitting Elias's prostate, making every nerve ending in Elias come alive.

"Fuck, Ty, please."

"I'm getting there," Ty said and licked the pre-come dribbling down Elias's dick. The sight of Ty going down on him was so torturous, Elias almost came right then and there.

Bending his knees, he dug his feet into the mattress. "Ty, I'm gonna come," he ground between clenched teeth.

"Not yet," Ty said, voice as tight as Elias's. Giving the tip of Elias's cock one last lick, he ripped into a condom packet, sheathed himself, and dripped lube down his length. Then he lined himself up at Elias's hole, looked up at him, and said, "Ready?"

"So ready," Elias said. He wrapped his legs around Ty's waist, heels digging into Ty's lower back.

The first breach of Ty's cock wasn't exactly painful, but it wasn't pleasant either. Elias gritted his teeth and bore down, knowing it would get easier once Ty's cock head got through.

"Hey. Eli, look at me."

He met Ty's gaze. Ty was sweating and breathing hard, but he still managed to shoot Elias a comforting smile, eyes bright.

"Relax," he said, massaging Elias's thighs again. "You're too tense. It'll hurt you if I keep going. Relax."

Closing his eyes, Elias released a slow breath and forced his body to do as Ty said—relax. Hands unfisted from the comforter, feet quit digging into Ty, back muscles unclenched —and Ty slipped in easily, as though Elias's body had sucked him in.

"Whoa," Elias rasped, eyes popping open. He'd never felt so full before, so connected to another person.

"Shit." Ty's eyes were squeezed shut, and a muscle ticked in his jaw, hands clenched on Elias's thighs. "Fuck, you're so tight."

"Haven't bottomed in over ten years," Elias admitted.

"Shit," Ty repeated with a weak chuckle. "Here I was trying not to come, and you go and say that?"

"Sorry?"

"No, you're not. Fuck you."

"Well, that's the idea."

Grinning, Ty moved then, eyes riveted on his own dick moving in and out of Elias. "Shit," he said yet again. "I wish you could see how hot this looks from here."

Elias had watched himself enter Ty numerous times in the past few weeks but never the opposite. Desperately wanting to see, he grabbed his pillow with a shaking hand and placed it under his head, lifting himself up. At this new angle, he had a decent view, but he wanted Ty's perspective. Groaning in a combination of frustration and pleasure, he let his head fall back as Ty continued his steady in-and-out rhythm.

"Harder, Ty."

Ty took him at his word and slammed back into him so hard it sent him scooting up the bed an inch.

"Yes, like that," he managed to utter. "Just like that." Ty slammed home again. "Fuck, yes. Don't stop."

Ty did stop but only for a few seconds. He let go of Elias's thigh with one hand and leaned over Elias's torso to brace it on the mattress. The other hand stayed on Elias's other thigh, keeping him spread open. Then he went to town.

And it was so good, so good, so good. Elias couldn't think, couldn't breathe, Ty's fast clip stealing his reasoning. The sound of Ty's balls hitting Elias's ass with every motion was loud in the room, revving him on further. Grasping his leaking dick, Elias pulled and squeezed.

A flush stole over Ty's cheekbones. He croaked, "I'm

coming," burying himself in Elias's ass and shuddering as he came, swearing beneath his breath. Elias finally let himself go and came all over his stomach.

Panting, abdomen painted in ropes of come, Elias let his legs fall to the bed. When Ty quit shaking, he gently withdrew from Elias, then got up to get rid of the condom. He came back from the bathroom with a warm washcloth and cleaned Elias up before crawling into bed and snuggling against him.

"Fuck, you're so hot."

Elias snorted. "You said that already."

"Bears repeating."

"You're going to give me a swelled head."

Ty laughed. Realizing what he'd said, Elias smiled too, even though he hadn't meant it that way.

They lay together, breaths evening out slowly. Elias ran his hand up and down Ty's sweaty back. His ass hurt a little but in an oh-so-good way. He was sated and loved and still buzzing off the endorphins. Knowing Ty would be asleep within seconds, Elias let his mind wander, trying to figure out the logistics of selling his place and moving to Ty's.

Moving to Ty's. Ty had asked him to move in with him, and Elias had jumped at the chance. It was insanely fast, completely stupid, and foolishly reckless.

Yet perfectly right.

Elias should've been freaking out and was honestly surprised that he wasn't. Back when he'd first been courting Ty—if offering up coffee and hot chocolate and apple turnovers could be considered courting—he'd done it partly because his advice column masquerading as a horoscope told him to be nice, partly because he felt bad for the way he'd treated Ty that first day, but also because blond, blue-eyed, boyishly handsome Ty had hit all of his buttons. Never in a million years would he have guessed that their first encounter would lead to the most important relationship of his life. Never would he have expected Ty to put up with a grumpy, emotionally-repressed fucker like him.

But for some stupid reason, Ty wanted him as much as he wanted Ty. Ty put up with his lack of communication better than anyone else ever had, although Elias had to admit to himself that he'd opened up to Ty more than he ever had to anyone else in his life except his adoptive parents. And that was all Ty's doing. His generous spirit, his understanding nature, his ability to see through Elias's walls... He made Elias feel safe.

Of course he was moving in with Ty. No way was he letting him get away ever.

"Ask you a question?"

Elias's entire body jerked. "Jesus!" he said. "You scared the shit out of me. I thought you were asleep."

"Are you kidding?" Ty lifted his head and rested it on his hand. His face was still slightly flushed, but his body had cooled down, and his breathing was back to normal. "There's way too much going on in my head."

Yeah, Elias could imagine. He wasn't feeling all that restful either. A lot of changes were happening at once. "What did you want to ask me?"

"I know I've been on you a lot lately," Ty said, fingers tracing Elias's collarbone, "about doing more with your photography than the few commissions you take and casually submitting photos to magazines. I just want to make sure that you took the job with *CanadaTravels* for you and not because you think it's something I want."

Elias took Ty's wrist and brought his hand up to kiss his palm. "I didn't take the job for you. I took it for me. This opportunity is the first time I've been excited about a job in a long time." He felt so *wanted* by the magazine. God, they'd tried for months to get him on board, despite his constant refusal. Damn if that didn't make him feel like a superhero. "But the reason I declined the VP offer at Top Line was partly because of you."

Ty's brow furrowed. "How so?"

"The VP job meant a raise, but it also meant more responsibility and a lot more travelling. If you think I'm glued to my phone now, if you think I work too much now, it would've been worse had I taken the job." He squeezed Ty's shoulder to get his boyfriend to look at him. "It would've taken me away from you too much, and I didn't want that. There'll be some travelling with the new job, but it won't be as often as it would've been had I taken the VP job."

Ty kissed Elias's chest. "But why quit? Why not stay in your current role?"

Sighing, Elias studied the pattern on the ceiling. "I never told you this, but shortly after we started seeing each other, I was tasked with firing a few people from a company we were reassessing." Ty tensed again him; Elias couldn't blame him. "I didn't want to, and the owner was going against our explicit recommendations, but I did my job. And afterwards? I felt like a fraud, and I was just...tired of looking into these unsuspecting people's faces and giving them bad news. I was so miserable with myself that I left work before lunch and spent the rest of the day on my couch watching TV and eating pancakes."

Ty snuggled closer, offering what support he could.

"I've been thinking about that a lot lately. I never like firing people, but lately it's been burning a hole in my soul. And I've realized you were right. These people, they didn't know they were about to be fired, which meant my argument about having job security at Top Line was invalid. Anything can change on a whim."

"I'm sorry you felt that way," Ty said. Elias looked at him, only to find a teasing glint in his ice-blue eyes. "You know, that's the most I've ever heard you speak in one go?"

"Yeah, it was exhausting," Elias had no trouble admitting. It made Ty laugh. "Oh! I have something for you." He untangled himself from Ty and headed for the kitchen.

"What is it?" Ty yelled from the bedroom.

"Just a little something," Elias called back from the kitchen.

"But we said no Valentine's Day presents!"

"It's nothing big." He walked back into the bedroom with his gift bag a few seconds later. "And it's not your typical Valentine's Day gift."

Ty held his hands out and waggled his fingers in a five-year-old's *gimme-gimme* gesture, the huge grin on his face making him *look* like said five-year-old. Elias handed him the bag with a laugh.

Grinning at the block of cheese he pulled out—Ty's favourite kind from the St. Lawrence Market—and a gift card to his favourite book store, the smile slipped off Ty's face when he removed the tissue paper from the five-by-seven picture frame. In it was a photo of a beardless and baby-faced twenty-two-year-old Elias, decked out in a graduation cap and gown, holding his Queen's University diploma, standing between his grinning parents. It was the same picture that stood on the dresser in Elias's living room. He knew Ty had noticed it, but he'd never asked about it, probably because he knew Elias tended to divulge things at his own pace.

"Eli," Ty whispered.

"Like I said, it's nothing big," Elias said. "But I know your whole family. I thought you'd like to meet mine."

Instant tears from Ty. His chin wobbled, wet eyes leaking, and he hugged the picture frame like it was a favored childhood Teddy bear. Elias had known how Ty might react, especially given how he'd reacted when Elias had gifted him with that picture on his birthday—the one of Ty in profile that now hung in Ty's living room.

It didn't look like Ty was going to let go of the frame any time soon, so Elias stretched out on his side and started talking.

"My mom was a principal at an elementary school. She was a sucker for anything apple flavoured and loved old western movies." He plucked at the comforter. It'd been so long since he'd talked about his parents, it was a relief to share them with someone. "My dad was a woodworker. He made this bed for me when I first got my own place. He loved Sandra Bullock movies and ABBA. It was his idea to take me to Disney World when they first adopted me."

Ty wiped his eyes and lay down next to him, setting the frame down between them. "Who's your favourite Disney character?"

Elias had to think about that one. "Mulan. She's badass."

"Mine're Timon and Pumba."

"Shocker."

"Thank you," Ty said, voice reedy. "For the gift and for sharing with me." His eyes held the questions Elias knew he wanted to ask.

"You can ask me about them any time," Elias assured him. "I like talking about them, remembering them."

"I don't have anything for you," Ty said. "A gift, I mean." *Because we said no gifts*, was left unsaid.

"Sure, you do. You offered me your home."

Ty smiled. "Oh yeah! And you said yes. Without an argument." He still sounded amazed by that. "I was thinking... You mentioned last week that the *CanadaTravels* job comes with a couple work-from-home days a week, so maybe we could convert the second bedroom into an office for you."

Elias ran his thumb over Ty's cheekbone, charmed by the offer. "Thank you, but I don't want to monopolize the bedroom. I was actually thinking I could convert that shed you've got out back."

Ty made a face. "The last owners used it as a chicken coop."

"Do you plan on getting chickens?"

"No," Ty said through a laugh. "But it still smells like a farm in there."

"Well, whatever. We'll figure it out."

Ty grunted and closed his eyes, settling in like he was finally about to take his post-orgasm nap, but then he snapped up to sitting with a gasp, startling Elias. "Wait! I *do* have a present for you." He smacked his forehead with a palm. "The chocolate syrup! I can't believe we didn't use it."

Elias laughed, making Ty smile wider. When their eyes met, they grinned stupidly at each other before launching themselves off the bed in a race to the kitchen to see who could get to the chocolate syrup first.

Chapter Fourteen

Ty expected to see stuffy old farts in suits at Top Line's VP's retirement party on Friday evening, sipping old scotch at the bar as they discussed the stock market. He got the suits and scotch and stock market right, but the very few stuffy old farts were interspersed with a mix of everyone from twenty-five to seventy with a high percentage of millennials.

This was so not his thing, attending a huge party where he only knew one person. Yet if large crowds weren't his thing, they were even less Elias's thing, and Ty felt a bit better knowing his boyfriend didn't want to be here either. It meant they wouldn't stay long.

"How about this?" Elias had said on the walk to the restaurant from the subway. "We eat some free food, have a drink, stay for the speeches, and once those are over and everybody swarms the bar, we sneak out the back."

"You know just how to turn me on," Ty had joked. It made Elias laugh.

Seated at a table in a corner nobody else had invaded yet, Ty munched on the mini quiche he'd plucked from the dinner buffet set out next to the bar. So far, he'd managed to avoid talking to anyone beyond the expected "Hi, nice to meet you," when Elias introduced him, but Elias wasn't so lucky. In the half hour they'd been here, he'd been stopped by no less than a dozen people expressing both disappointment that he was leaving Top Line and well wishes in his new job.

Speaking with his colleagues, Elias was cool and confident. Dressed in a charcoal suit, white shirt, and purple tie, he was so drool-worthy that Ty was still surprised Elias had picked *him* to plan a life with. He hadn't planned on asking Elias to move in with him so soon, but it had seemed like all the pieces had fallen into place on Valentine's Day. He couldn't not take the chance.

"I did reconnaissance," Elias said in his ear, sitting down on the bench seat next to Ty with a full plate of food. Ty shivered at the caress of Elias's warm breath against his skin. "The back exit is at the end of that hallway." Elias gestured toward the hallway that also led to the restrooms. "From what I've been able to gather, there are three speeches: the president, the VP, and the new VP. The president's EA said they're about ten minutes each, and they should be starting in the next few minutes, which means we should be able to sneak out of here in about forty minutes, and we can be home in an hour if we cab it."

"God bless you." Ty toasted him with his beer bottle.

"And check out what I found." Elias placed a series of mini chocolate goodies on Ty's plate. "They brought out the desserts already."

Ty abandoned the real food on his plate and popped a mini brownie in his mouth. Moaning in appreciation, he smiled when Elias fidgeted. He ate a second dessert and repeated the moan. Elias fidgeted again. Good. Maybe if he got Elias horny enough, they could screw the speeches, leave sometime in the next few seconds, and go home to screw each other instead.

"Elias, hey."

Damn, plan aborted.

Rachel, Elias's colleague whom Ty had met a couple weeks ago at the St. Lawrence Market, sat across from them, her husband to her right.

Elias cleared his throat. "Hey, Rachel, Aric."

Hands shaken and re-introductions made, Rachel looked around the packed restaurant. "I swear I see more people here that I don't know than those I do, and I know everybody in our office."

"Clients and board members are here, too," Elias explained.

"What do you think?" Rachel asked. "Should we do something similar for your going-away party?"

Elias paled underneath his brown skin. Rachel laughed all the way to the buffet line. Ty couldn't help but enjoy her sense of humor.

"She's not serious, is she?" Elias asked Aric.

"Eh." Aric shrugged like, *maybe, maybe not*. "If she invites you to any meetings in the next couple of weeks, I'd decline."

"Great."

At one of the more crowded tables, an older woman with dyed-auburn hair wearing a plaid skirt and white blouse stood and clinked her spoon against her water glass.

"Thank you everyone for coming out tonight," she said once the room had quieted, her British accent soft. "It's been an honor working with each and every one of you over the last twenty-five years—"

Ty tuned her out. Instead, he used his fork to scoop the icing off his mini cupcake. There was more icing than cupcake, and really, that was just gross. Unless it was Maddie's icing, he didn't want it on his dessert.

Rachel returned with two plates of desserts. Setting them down in the middle of the table, she pushed one closer to Ty with a wink. Ty grinned his thanks and nabbed the brownies.

The speeches went on for close to forever, and by the time they were done, Ty's stomach was full of too many desserts, and he wasn't feeling so good. It was easy to forget how much junk he was eating when the food was bitesized.

Just as Elias had predicted, as soon as the speeches were over, everybody herded to the bar like a cackle of starving hyenas. It was so time to make their escape. Ty couldn't wait to get his tie off.

Elias squeezed his thigh. "I'm going to use the restroom, and then we can go."

Ty might not have been feeling a hundred percent, but that didn't prevent him from checking out his boyfriend's tight ass as he walked away.

"I still can't believe he's leaving," Rachel said. "I thought he'd be a Top Line lifer."

"Nah," Ty said. "He wasn't happy there."

Rachel's smile was sad. "Yeah, he told me. I didn't even know he was into photography and then all of a sudden he has a job as the director of one at the country's number one travel magazine?"

"Have you seen his website?" Ty asked.

"He has a website?" Rachel tossed her hands in the air. "Seriously, three years we've worked together, and I feel like I don't know him at all. You two have been dating for, like, five minutes and already you know more than me."

Yeah, Elias wasn't exactly a sharer. That he'd opened up to Ty so much in the past few weeks was a minor miracle.

Aric patted his wife's hand where it rested on the table-top. "Not everyone wears their heart on their sleeve like you, honey."

"Well, they should," Rachel grumbled. "Life would be a lot easier that way."

"Oh my God," Ty said in horror. "The world would be a madhouse."

Rachel laughed before taking a sip of her wine. "Tell me Ty," she said, twirling her glass on the table. "Are you a Capricorn?"

"I am." He wasn't surprised by the question; Elias had told him about Rachel's fascination with what she called "the spiritual" and Elias called "hocus pocus bullshit."

She nodded. "I thought as much." When he raised an eyebrow in question, she waved a hand in the air. "Oh, just based on something Elias asked me a while back about a Capricorn dating a Capricorn."

Ty rubbed a hand over his mouth to cover his smirk. Elias might call it "hocus pocus bullshit," but Ty suspected that, deep down, he actually believed in it a little bit. Why else would he humour Rachel's need to know his horoscope every morning?

"What is it that you do, Ty?" Aric asked.

"Yeah," Rachel said. "When I asked Elias last week, he said you work for the city but couldn't remember what you do exactly."

Desserts curdling in his stomach, Ty's hand spasmed on his water glass, smile freezing on his face. Elias couldn't remember that he swapped out full garbage bags for empty ones in street trash cans within a four-block radius in the downtown core? It wasn't fucking rocket science.

Rachel was still waiting for an answer, so he told her the truth. He wasn't sure what he expected, censure or disgust or indifference. What he got was a casual, "Cool. Do you work in the Bay and King area? If so, we should get lunch sometime, or coffee."

Aric snorted. "Don't mind her," he said to Ty. "She can't help trying to make new friends wherever she goes."

Rachel ribbed her husband back, but Ty was too numb to pay attention.

Elias reappeared, finished off the last of his beer, and said, "Ready to go?"

Winter coats were put on, and goodbyes must've surely been made, but it happened in a haze, and the next thing Ty knew, he was in a cab with Elias, staring out the window, watching the city lights go by, the snow gently falling to the ground, bundled-up pedestrians rushing to Friday night activities. Next to him, Elias checked emails on his phone.

Obviously, Elias had been busy. When Rachel had asked about what Ty did for a living, Elias must've been in the middle of something and told her he didn't remember so that she wouldn't pry, and he could get back to his work.

Right?

Because the only other explanation he could think of made him feel about two inches tall.

They were walking into Elias's condo fifteen minutes later. Cold all over despite the condo's warmth, Ty kept his coat on and wrapped his arms around himself.

"I think there's still some chocolate syrup left," Elias said, heading for the kitchen. "What do you say?" Turning to walk backwards so that he faced Ty, he waggled his eyebrows suggestively. When Ty didn't smile back, when he didn't move from the front entrance, Elias frowned and headed back to him. "What's wrong?"

Ty couldn't meet his eyes, and his gaze drifted down the hallway, to the kitchen, to the TV in the living room. Anywhere except at Elias. The feeling growing more and more solid in his gut made him grit his teeth against the words that wanted to escape. He needed to know, but he was afraid of the answer.

"Are you embarrassed of me?" he finally asked.

Elias's eyes went wide, and he took a half-step back. "What?" He sounded surprised and wounded by the question. "Why would you even ask me that?" The disbelief in his tone had Ty believing Elias wasn't embarrassed about him, but Rachel's words still niggled at him.

"I was talking to Rachel while you were in the restroom," Ty said. Elias's shrug said, *So what?* "She said she asked you what I do for a living...and that you said you *couldn't remember*?" His voice turned incredulous there at the end, because what the fuck?

Something in Elias's eyes shifted and Ty's heart sank, the bottom falling out of his stomach.

"Oh my God," he rasped, eyes burning. "You are embarrassed of me."

"I am *not* embarrassed by you, Ty." Elias's voice held no give. Ty was inclined to believe him given that he'd taken Ty to a work function and introduced him around, but if he hadn't told Rachel what he did for a living, it meant...

"My job," Ty realized. He swallowed past the knot in his throat, refusing to cry in front of cool-as-a-rock Elias. "You're embarrassed by my job."

Elias opened his mouth to answer, closed it without saying anything. He shifted on the spot and glanced away.

Releasing a bark of unamused laughter, Ty shook his head, the desserts he'd eaten threatening to make a reappearance via his mouth. "You are." His heart hurt too much to speak past an agonized whisper.

"Ty—"

"Oh, that's rich." Now he found volume. "You *fire* people for a living, and you're embarrassed by *my* job?"

"Ty, I..."

He waited. For a "Let me explain," or "You've got it all wrong," or "You misunderstood," or even an "You're right, I'm sorry." The longer he waited, the spikier the ball of hurt and resentment grew in his chest, raking painful slashes into his sternum. A lump the size of a fist choked off his words, a good thing given nothing good would come out if he opened his mouth to speak right now. He gave Elias a few more seconds to explain. When nothing was forthcoming, Ty squared his shoulders and walked out.

Chapter Fifteen

Of course, everything went to shit. Just like that doom and gloom feeling that had been plaguing Elias for the past few days had predicted. Ty was gone. And it was all Elias's fault.

It was just that the question, *Are you embarrassed about my job?*, had thrown him, because the truth was no. He wasn't. But once upon a time—hell, as early as this morning—he had been. Fuck if that didn't make him feel petty and insecure and self-righteous.

Had Ty asked him that question a month ago, Elias would've dodged as best he could, because the answer would've hurt Ty. *Yes, I am embarrassed about your job. You can do so much better.* God, when had Elias become so judgemental and disapproving? He'd come from nothing and worked his way up; who was he to judge how others chose to live their lives?

The truth was that he wasn't embarrassed by Ty's job. He was embarrassed of *himself*. But before he could sort out those thoughts in his head and articulate them to Ty, his boyfriend had left. Elias couldn't blame him. He'd stood there like a dead fish while Ty waited for an answer. Ty was hurt and angry and confused, no doubt wondering why he put up with Elias's bullshit at all.

The room spun around him, and he sagged against the back of the couch, pressing a fist against his aching heart. What if Ty decided Elias wasn't worth it? What if he couldn't fix things between them, and Ty never came back? What if Rachel had been right all those weeks ago, when she'd implied that a Capricorn and a Capricorn weren't a good match for each other? Was this the catalyst for the end of them, for what astrology said wouldn't work anyway?

He had no idea what to do. Did he give Ty space to calm down? Did he run after him, get to him before he reached his car in the building's parking garage, got in, and drove away, possibly for good? Did he text him an apology, an explanation? Call him?

Fuck, relationships were complicated. No wonder he avoided them, but he wasn't going to let this...this...disagreement, argument, *whatever*, keep them apart.

Getting online, he typed *what to do when a capricorn is angry* into Google. Theoretically Elias should know the answer to that given that he himself was a Capricorn, but Ty wasn't a typical Capricorn, and he was at a loss.

General consensus number one: When a Capricorn gets angry, they become cold and even more withdrawn into themselves.

True for Elias. False for Ty, who had no problem letting Elias know how he felt.

General consensus number two: Capricorns tend to use logic instead of emotions when they're upset, honesty that cut like knives.

Yeah, that was certainly true.

You fire people for a living and you're embarrassed by my job?

Elias couldn't deny the truth of those words.

General consensus number three: Behind the cool, reserved, logical front of a Capricorn lies an incredibly sensitive and attentive heart.

Again, true for Elias, yet though Ty was extremely logical, he was the least cool and reserved person Elias knew. Unlike Elias he wasn't afraid to let his sensitive and caring nature show.

General consensus number four: Not all Capricorns are the same.

Well, no fucking shit. He didn't need the fucking internet to tell him that. He just had to look at the personality differences between Ty and himself to piece that together. Ty's birthday was almost at the end of the Capricorn cycle. Maybe that meant he had some qualities of whatever the next sign was. He typed *what sign comes after Capricorn?* into Google but shut his laptop without looking at the search results. It would probably confuse him even more than he already was.

Besides, he didn't fail to notice that not a single website told him how to deal with an angry Capricorn, and that was useless.

And okay, maybe he was going about it all wrong, looking at Ty as this *thing* he had to solve, lumped into a whole like he was part of a hive mind instead of the individual person he was. As Elias's boyfriend, who was smart and funny and generous and warm. Everything Elias wasn't.

The last time Ty had been upset with him had been weeks ago, right after they'd started seeing each other. Elias had asked him why he didn't get his GED, so he could go to college or university and get a better, higher paying job. Ty had been upset and not afraid to show it, and Elias had been honest about his ignorance then apologized. Ty had forgiven and forgotten.

Simple as that: honesty and apology. It was so clear now that it was exactly what Ty had been waiting for from Elias earlier.

Decided, Elias grabbed his keys and his coat and left the condo.

By the time Ty parked his car in his parents' driveway twenty minutes after leaving Elias's, the snow was falling in earnest, big, fat flakes perfect for making snowballs. If only his stupid boyfriend was around, so he could throw one at his sanctimonious head and knock some sense into it.

That was a mean thought, and he felt bad having it, but though the resentment and anger had faded during the drive, he was still hurt and sad and feeling all kinds of guilty for walking out on Elias.

Literally everybody in Elias's life had left him. His mom took off, his dad died in prison, his adoptive parents died in a plane crash, his best friend moved to Ireland, his sister was across the country. And there Ty was, doing the same thing, walking away when he should've stayed. Hadn't he promised himself weeks ago that he'd be the one to prove to Elias that not everybody left?

But God, he'd just been so upset that he hadn't wanted to stick around for fear he'd say something he'd regret. That last quip he'd thrown at Elias before walking out was bad enough.

This was the second time Elias had made him feel small about his job, and he didn't know what to do about it. How were they supposed to move forward if Elias couldn't respect him? For the love of God, he'd asked Elias to move in with him. How were they supposed to make things work with this giant elephant between them?

Sighing, he turned off the car and trudged up the snowy steps to his parents' front door. There weren't any other cars in the driveway, so maybe nobody was home. Please let that be the case. He could crash on the couch in the basement and maybe his mom would make him French toast and bacon for breakfast tomorrow morning.

Though he'd miss Elias's Saturday morning pancakes. His eyes burned, but he refused to shed any tears over a *boy*, no siree. Jenn's anguished teenaged voice from long-ago wailed in his head: "I'm not going to cry over a stupid boy. Boys are dumb!"

Ty could say with confidence that yes, she'd been right—boys were dumb.

It was warm inside the house but not as quiet as he'd expected. The TV was on and there was the sound of crackly peanut shells being forced open. His dad appeared in the hallway as Ty was taking off his boots.

"Hey, Dad."

"Hey, Ty. Everything okay?"

Not so much.

"Where're Mom and Maddie?" he asked instead of answering.

His dad shrugged. "Maddie could be at the movies or in the North Pole for all I know. Your mom's at one of her committee planning sessions."

Ty ignored his dad's narrowed eyes and concentrated on hanging his winter coat in the closet, smoothing down the creases so it hung just so.

"What's going on, Ty? What's happened?"

Clearly Ty's attempt at nonchalance was a huge failure.

"Dad, I made a huge mistake."

A FEW MINUTES LATER, TY SIPPED HIS HOT CHOCOLATE AND moaned when the warm drink hit his belly. He didn't need more chocolate; the desserts from the party earlier still sat like indigestible rocks in his stomach, but his dad had made it for him, and he couldn't say no to that.

He was still in his uncomfortable monkey suit, but he'd finally removed his tie and suit jacket. Next to him, his dad leaned back on his elbows on the stair above him. For as long as Ty could remember, the bottom of the staircase had been their place to talk.

"If I've got this straight," his dad said, "the mistake was asking Elias to move in with you?"

"No! Of course not!"

"Okay, so you still want him to move in with you?" His dad sounded like he was trying to make heads or tails of Ty's admittedly rushed explanation of recent events, concluding with tonight's argument.

"Yes, more than anything." Ty cupped both hands around his hot mug and let it warm him up. "The mistake was walking away tonight, when I should've stayed."

His dad was silent for a minute, probably gathering the words in his head, just like Ty sometimes had to do. Sitting up, he leaned his elbows on his knees, mimicking Ty's position.

"Walking away from an argument won't solve anything," he said. "But sometimes it's necessary, and that's not a bad thing. Especially if it stops you from saying something you might not be able to take back later."

Somehow his dad's words didn't make Ty feel any better. He didn't want Elias to think that he was leaving forever. He just needed space. He should've said so before walking out without a word.

Fuck, he was a gigantic jackass.

His dad patted his knee. "I'm sorry you're fighting, kiddo."

"We're not fighting really. It's more of an impasse."

"Consider it from his perspective, Ty. From what you've told me about his past, he's probably worked really hard to get to where he is today. He seems like the kind of person who has a plan for how his life will go and what he'll do and probably even the type of person he'd end up making a life with." Elias was exactly that type of person. Ty remembered having the same thought weeks ago. "Maybe what you do for a living didn't factor into his plans, but...he's with you anyway, isn't he?"

True. Yes, that was true.

"Consider also that he might be feeling just like you: hurt and resentful."

Ty frowned into his mug. "What do you mean?"

"Well, you say he's embarrassed about your job. That makes you feel pretty shitty, doesn't it? But didn't you tell me a few weeks ago that you don't like his either?"

Ty froze with his mug halfway to his lips, prickly fingers of shame wicking up his spine. Fuck him, his dad was right, so completely right. At least Elias had had the foresight to keep his feelings about Ty's job to himself, whereas Ty hadn't been shy letting Elias know that his job sucked, which must've made Elias feel like utter crap.

Gigantic jackass over here, ladies and gentlemen.

"Shit," he whispered. Setting his mug down on the floor, he buried his face in his hands. "Fuck, Dad, I'm such a hypocrite!"

"*And*—" His dad kept going as if Ty hadn't spoken, as if his whole perspective hadn't just been flipped on its axis. "—didn't you just tell me that you got a new job? Elias too? So really, you're arguing over nothing."

"You're saying this argument is stupid?" Ty asked.

"Not stupid. But maybe unnecessary. Pointless. Moot."

"A moo point, like a cow's opinion?"

"No, *moot*," his dad said, extra emphasis on the *t*, his expression asking Ty what dummy thought a cow had an opinion. "M-o-o-t."

Despite how unfunny this situation with Elias was, Ty chuckled weakly. "No, I know. I was just making a lame joke." Clearly his dad had never watched an episode of *Friends*. Sighing, he rested his temple against the staircase railing. "I owe Eli such an apology."

"Don't put it off." His dad patted his knee again before getting up. "Call him now, before things get weird."

Headlights illuminated the living room through the gaps in the closed curtains, tires crunching snow. Ty secretly hoped it wasn't his mom. He so wasn't in the mood for a Sue Green inquiry.

"Your mom must be back early," his dad said, moving to the living room, where he fingered the curtain aside and peered out. Ty checked his watch for the time. God, only eight-thirty. So much had happened tonight; it felt closer to midnight.

"Does Elias drive a big, black SUV?"

Ty's heart jumpstarted in his chest, and butterflies tickled his stomach. "Eli's here?"

"Mm-hmm. Just got out of the car. Looks like you'll be able to give that apology sooner than you thought."

"But I'm not ready! I don't know what to say!"

"Sometimes you just have to wing it, kiddo."

The look Ty shot his dad must've been pretty pathetic, because his dad sighed, rolled his eyes, and put on his boots.

"You've got five minutes," he said, shrugging on his coat.

But Ty stopped him before he could open the door.

———

THANK GOD TY'S CAR WAS PARKED IN HIS PARENTS' driveway. Once Elias had reached his own car, he hadn't given himself much time to make a decision: head to Ty's parents or to Ty's house. Ty's parents were much closer, so Elias had gone on instinct and headed here. The relief that Ty hadn't driven the hour-plus home to Puslinch on a dangerously snowy night was immense.

But as he watched Ty's dad exit the house, a fist of anxiety closed around his throat. Was this where Mr. Green would tell him that Ty didn't want to see him anymore and to remove himself from the premises immediately before he got his shotgun?

Okay, he might've exaggerated the scenario a little bit, but the fear that Ty would tell him to fuck off forever hadn't gone away on the drive here, so to say he was surprised when Mr. Green held out a hand to him was a vast understatement.

"Elias, it's good to see you." Mr. Green even offered a genuine smile. Elias couldn't manage to smile back, but he shook Mr. Green's hand briefly. Yet before he could let go, Mr. Green used the opportunity to pull Elias toward the sidewalk. "Walk with me for a few minutes," he said, dropping Elias's hand.

Elias looked back at the house, where Ty surely was.

"Don't worry about him," Mr. Green said as they walked, their steps leaving footprints in the snow behind them. "He'll be there when we get back."

"He must be pretty mad at me." Elias's hands balled into fists in his coat pockets.

Mr. Green zipped his jacket up against the cold. "Not really."

Elias didn't buy that for a second.

"Ty didn't, uh..." Mr. Green cleared his throat and blinked against the fat snowflakes falling from the sky. "What was I supposed to say?" he muttered. Elias didn't think he was supposed to hear that part. "Right, uh, Elias, Ty might've left your place because he was angry, but he didn't leave *you*."

When they reached the stop sign at the end of the quiet street, Elias turned to him. "Did Ty tell you to tell me that?"

Mr. Green scoffed. "*No.*" A little less emphasis might've made that more convincing. "No, no, we were just, ah, talking, and it came up, so I thought I would...reassure you."

Elias blinked at him. A spot of colour darkened Mr. Green's cheekbones, and he fidgeted on his feet. "You're really bad at this," Elias concluded.

Mr. Green's laugh lines became more prominent when he chuckled. "Yeah, I know." He clapped Elias on the shoulder. "Don't tell Ty."

They headed back to the house in silence, the only sound coming from the snow crunching under their feet and shovels hitting pavement as some of the neighbours shovelled their driveways. Despite the hopeless feeling in his gut when he'd arrived, he couldn't help being a little bit amused that Ty had sent his dad out here to comfort him. The question was, why hadn't Ty come out himself? The words would've been much more reassuring from him.

The man himself was standing next to a three feet tall, lopsided snowman in the yard when Elias and Mr. Green arrived back at the house. A snowman that hadn't been there when Elias had arrived five minutes ago. Dressed in the wool coat he'd had on when he'd left Elias's—Elias sort of missed his ugly, puffy, white one—Ty smiled tentatively. The snowman had a curved piece of wood as a mouth, no nose, and thumb depressions for eyes. Its wooden stick arms stuck out straight in front of him, holding a small piece of cardboard with the words *I'm sorry* scribbled in black marker. Elias smiled as relief hit. Hope was not lost.

Mr. Green snorted. Ty glared at his dad and pointed at the house. Mr. Green left, a wide grin on his face.

Elias took a deep breath. "Ty, I'm sorry—"

"No." Ty held out a gloved hand palm-out in the universal *stop* gesture. "*I'm* sorry."

"You don't have anything to apologize for," Elias said.

"Oh, I do," Ty countered. "Starting with..." He paused, and even in the dark Elias saw him swallow hard. "I'm so sorry I left."

His voice could barely be heard over the song-o-shovels. Despising the distance between them, Elias joined him on the snow-covered lawn, not stopping until he was less than a foot away.

"I was embarrassed that you're embarrassed by me," Ty continued. "I left because I didn't want to say anything bad that I couldn't take back."

"Ty." Elias placed his hands on Ty's cheeks. His fingers were gloveless and must've been cold on Ty's face, but Ty didn't flinch. "I'm not embarrassed by you, or your job." Ty flicked his eyes away, and Elias knew he had to work harder. "I used to be," he admitted. Those blue eyes came back to him. In the pale glow of the porch light, they were darker than normal. Running his hands down Ty's arms, he laced his fingers with Ty's gloved ones. "Ever since I was a kid, I wanted to be better than my birth parents. Better than a mom who left and a dad who sold drugs to kids. I had this vision of what my life would be like: good school, good job, good money, a nice home, eventually a good guy with a good job, and we'd live a good life together." He snorted at his own naiveté. "Sounds perfectly boring, doesn't it?"

"No," Ty whispered. "It sounds nice."

"But instead," he continued, voice matching Ty's, "I met the perfect guy with a great job he loves. Yeah, at first I was embarrassed by your job, but now I'm just embarrassed at myself because of this stupid, outdated ideal in my head of the type of guy I should end up with, and I let it colour how I felt about your work. It was insensitive and idealistic, and I apologize." He squeezed Ty's fingers. "It's what I should've said earlier, but I couldn't get the words out."

But Ty was shaking his head. "Eli, you don't get it. If anyone's been insensitive, it's me. At least you had the decency to spare my feelings by not telling me what you thought about my job. I was an ass." He chuckled without humour. "I had no reservations in letting you know how I felt about your job. I must've made you feel awful, and you never called me out on it."

Elias shrugged. "Because you were right. My job sucks." He laughed because he could say that now and not feel like he was betraying both himself and Top Line. "I do fire people for a living."

Ty winced. "I'm sorry I said that."

"No." Elias finally gave in to what he wanted and pressed his cold lips to Ty's. Ty snuggled closer, arms wrapping around Elias's back. Elias didn't mean to let it go further than lips against lips, but Ty gasped, and he couldn't help taking advantage of that open mouth. Licking his way inside Ty's mouth, he tasted chocolate, and his full-body shiver had nothing to do with the cold. Yet this kiss wasn't about sex. It was about comfort and apology and love and a need to feel close to Ty again.

"No," Elias repeated when he pulled back, hands cupping Ty's neck, thumbs tracing cheeks heated from the kiss. Snowflakes glittered on his eyelashes and in his hair. "You said everything I needed to hear about my work. That I wasn't happy and that I was too talented a photographer to let it go to waste. And the truth is, if I hadn't met you, if I were single right now and had been offered the VP job? I would've taken it, and I would've been a repressed, miserable motherfucker for the rest of my life."

Ty chuckled and moved in for a hug, burying his face in Elias's neck. "I'm sorry," he breathed against Elias's skin, warm breath a contrast to the cold winter air.

"I'm sorry, too," Elias said. "I love you, Ty." Inhaling deeply, he memorized the scent of Ty: pine-scented soap over a subtle layer of chocolate. He held him tighter, knowing his outdated ideals could've cost him this wonderful man who saw past Elias's walls to the heart of who he was.

"I love you, too. I won't walk away like that again," Ty promised.

"That would be nice."

Ty pulled back with a grin. "You know, my dad made a good point earlier. He said that we both got new jobs, so our argument was moot anyway."

"Huh, that is a good point. Don't I feel like an idiot?"

Ty snorted a laugh.

"Speaking of your dad," Elias said. "Did you send him out here to tell me that stuff?"

"What? *No.*" Ty took a step out of Elias's arms and avoided Elias's gaze. The fact that he didn't ask, "What stuff?" was a bit of a giveaway. How would he know what they'd discussed unless he'd sent his dad out here with specific instructions? "Of course not. He just wanted to come out here and talk to you."

Uh-huh. "God, you're as bad as your dad."

Ty's shoulders slumped. "Yeah, I know. I just needed a few minutes to gather my thoughts."

"I figured."

"And to make my snowpal."

Elias peered around Ty, where the little snowman still held the *I'm sorry* sign. Its mouth had fallen off at some point. "You know, that's the creepiest snowman I've ever seen."

"Shhh." Ty covered its fake ears—or where its fake ears would be if it had any. "Fluffy Snowdrift will hear you," he whisper-shouted.

"He doesn't even have any eyes. He looks like a reject from *The Nightmare Before Christmas.*"

Ty lost it, laughing so long and hard the sound echoed up and down the street. A few houses down a dog started to bark. Coming around Fluffy Snowdrift, he launched himself at Elias. Heart fluttering, Elias caught him close and kissed his cheek, marveling at the way their evening had gone from agonizingly awful to so, so right.

"Hey," Elias said. "I just realized. You never apologized that first day."

Ty pulled back to frown at him. "What first day?"

"The day we met. Remember? When you lectured me about which garbage can to throw my newspaper in?"

"What?" The look of disbelief on Ty's face was hilarious. "Why would I apologize for that? Had you put it in the right garbage can in the first place, I wouldn't have said anything." *And we never would've met*, was left unsaid, though Elias was sure they were both thinking it. "Recycling isn't a game, you know," Ty continued, the twinkle in those ice blue eyes belying the serious set of his face. "It's extremely important for the environment—"

Elias tuned Ty out as he started talking about glass plants and plastic plants and what-the-fuck-ever plants, just like he had on the day they'd met. To shut him up, Elias used a technique he never would've considered then.

He kissed the shit out of him.

Thank you for coming along on Ty and Elias's journey.

If you enjoyed the book please consider leaving some stars or a review on Amazon, Goodreads, or your favourite review site. Every review helps!

To keep up-to-date on my new releases, and for early access to cover reveals and teasers as well as weekly and monthly giveaways, join my Facebook Group, Amy Aislin's Readers.

And don't forget that you can find bonus content for all of my books on my website at www.amyaislin.com/bonus-content. Character artwork, teasers, excerpts, and blog posts, all in one place.

About the Author

Amy's lived with her head in the clouds since she first picked up a book as a child, and being fluent in two languages means she's read *a lot* of books! She first picked up a pen on a rainy day in fourth grade when her class had to stay inside for recess. Tales of treasure hunts with her classmates eventually morphed into love stories between men, and she's been writing ever since. She writes evenings and weekends—or whenever she isn't at her full-time day job saving the planet at Canada's largest environmental non-profit.

An unapologetic introvert, Amy reads too much and socializes too little, with no regrets. She loves connecting with readers. Join her Facebook Group, Amy Aislin's Readers, to stay up-to-date on upcoming releases and for access to early teasers, find her on Instagram and Twitter, or sign up for her newsletter.

www.amyaislin.com

 instagram.com/amyaislin

 facebook.com/amy.aislin

 twitter.com/amy_aislin

 bookbub.com/profile/amy-aislin